A Different Kind of Beauty

SYLVIA McNICOLL

10 9 8 7 6 5 4 3 2

National Library of Canada Cataloguing in Publication

McNicoll, Sylvia, 1954-
A different kind of Beauty / by Sylvia McNicoll.

Sequel to: Bringing up Beauty.
ISBN 1-55005-059-1 (bound).—ISBN 1-55005-060-5 (pbk.)

I. Title.   PS8575.N52D53 2003   jC813'.54   C2003-902341-9
PZ7

U.S. Publisher Cataloging-in-Publication Data
(Library of Congress Standards)

McNicoll, Sylvia, 1954 -
A different kind of beauty / Sylvia McNicoll.—1st ed.
[   ] p. : cm.
Summary: The relationship between a dog and a man
who is coping with his impending blindness.
Sequel to: Bringing up beauty.
ISBN 1-55005-059-1
ISBN 1-55005-060-5 (pbk.)
1. Guide dogs _ Fiction _ Juvenile literature.
2. Human-animal relationships -_ Fiction _ Juvenile literature.
(1. Guide dogs _ Fiction. 2. Human-animal relationships -_ Fiction.)
I. Title.   [Fic] 21   PZ7.M2385Di 2003

Fitzhenry & Whiteside acknowledges with thanks the Canada Council
for the Arts, the Government of Canada through the Book Publishing
Industry Development Program (BPIDP), the Ontario Arts Council and
the Government of Ontario through the Ontario Media Development
Corporation's Ontario Book Initiative for their support
for our publishing program.

Cover Illustration by Sharif Tarabay
Design by Wycliffe Smith Design Inc.
Printed in Canada

A Different Kind of Beauty

SYLVIA McNICOLL

FITZHENRY & WHITESIDE

DEDICATION

For Angela McKay who lost her sight and gained a vision.

ACKNOWLEDGEMENT

For all the insights and information, thank you to Angela McKay & Fenway, Karolyn Al-Koura & Silver, Lori Shea & Karoo, Canine Vision Canada and the Canadian National Institute for the Blind; also,thank you to Dr. Lindsay MacVicar for the medical facts checkup. Another special thank you to Kate Lowe and her grade six class for listening to the story and to my daughter Jennifer for reading Elizabeth's half to them. There are many tales and truths that went into the making of *A Different Kind of Beauty*. However, in the end I folded, stapled and mutilated them all for the sake of fiction. Any errors made are entirely my own.

Thank you also to The Canada Council for the Arts who always help me when I ask. I am deeply grateful as well for the many library visits across the country the Council has sponsored on my behalf. I feel lucky to be Canadian.

CHAPTER 1

Elizabeth and Beauty

Debra's Home Again

Fall—you gotta love it. At least Beauty sure did. Bright white sunshine that warmed the frost from her paws. Crisp breezy air that cooled her down enough for long walks. And swishy orange-brown leaves that carried delicious smells she couldn't resist—and which she added to, by squatting. With every happy step her thick brown tail waved "hello": to the bright red cardinal trilling in the tree; to the squirrel she strained at the leash for. I had to yank her back for that one. A future guide dog can't chase squirrels. Was she ever going to learn?

Hello to the cat squinting from behind a picture window. Beauty's tail was waving again. Hello to my former and only boyfriend, Scott, walking on the sidewalk with his latest girlfriend. I wanted to die when I saw her.

"Hi, Elizabeth," Scott called to me, not dropping the hand of the blonde beside him. She seemed to grip his hand more tightly as she smiled at me too.

"Hi, Scott."

Beauty angled herself so she could lick Scott's out-stretched hand while slapping The Girlfriend's legs with her tail.

Why did I feel like saying, *Good girl, Beauty*, instead of what I really said? "Settle down, Beauty. C'mon now. Settle down."

"Gwen, this is my friend Elizabeth and her dog Beauty the Second."

"Oooh, kind of like royalty, eh?" She reached out and patted Beauty's head. "Is she a chocolate Lab?"

"Mm-hmm." Beauty's brown fur and pink-rimmed nose and eyes were a dead giveaway.

"Elizabeth fosters Labs for the Lions Foundation," Scott told her. I liked the way he said that, as though he was proud of me. "They train dogs for blind people."

"So does that mean you have to give her back to...um... that foundation?" She scratched behind Beauty's ears now.

I nodded. "But I still have at least five months with her."

"How could you ever give up such a cute puppy-wuppy?" she baby-talked at Beauty. Beauty dropped her mouth into a grin, agreeing with Gwen as she slurped at her hand.

"I've done it before with Beauty One. Knowing that she's not mine, I hold back a little." I smiled and looked at Scott. It was kind of the way I felt toward him. We'd been best friends forever and went out for a while when he still went to my school. Scott made me laugh and always put me in a good mood, just like Beauty. But he belongs to everybody; he's just that friendly. I have to hold back every time I see him.

"I could never do that," Gwen said with awe. Beauty twisted her head and leaned toward Gwen to get a better angle for ear scratching.

"Once you see your dog guiding a blind person, it makes it all worthwhile." Suddenly, I wanted to explain more to Gwen, about how this time I wouldn't let myself get sick over giving up Beauty. I would eat normal meals, not just dry toast. I'd drink milk, not flat ginger ale. And I wouldn't cry over her old toys. This Beauty would be different. Instead I repeated, "The blind person makes it all worthwhile."

"Her fur is so smooth and shiny," Gwen said as she patted her.

Funny she should admire that about Beauty when I envied that very thing about Gwen. Her hair looked like wheat hanging upside down, blond and straight. My hair kind of sproinged from my head, all red and bushy. Gwen's skin looked smooth too—no two-million freckles to play connect-the-dots with.

"Beauty does amazing tricks." Scott dropped to his knees now. "C'mon girl, do Elvis for Gwen." Scott started singing, slightly off key, *"You ain't nothin' but a hound dog…"* He tossed back his head and howled, "Arr-rooo!"

Beauty's upper lip hooked over her left incisor as she gave a soft growl. She wagged her whole body and Scott wagged his butt. They howled together. With a stretch of the imagination you could see how she sort of looked like Elvis, with her wagging butt and curled lip; at least like the Elvis I'd watched on Dad's old videos.

"Uh, thank you, thank you very much," I said in my best southern drawl. It was Beauty's cue to stop. Her lip sank down again.

"That is amazing," Gwen said, chuckling.

"Elizabeth's great with animal training," Scott agreed as he stood up.

"Hey, I never did anything. Beauty came by her Elvis naturally," I said.

"Actually, I think Beauty's training you, Scott!" Gwen touched his arm. Did she know about us—I mean, the former us?

"Well, nice to meet you, Gwen. We've gotta go. We're picking up Debra from the airport and I just wanted to tire Beauty out. She gets restless in the car," I told Scott. "My sister's flying in from L.A.," I explained to Gwen.

"Is she an actress?" Gwen asked, sounding hopeful.

"No. Even better. She's a famous artist. Debra Kerr. She illustrated *Camel on a Skateboard*. I'm sure you've heard of it."

Gwen's blue eyes lit up instantly. "My little sister has that book! Wow, that's really exciting! Maybe I can pop by and get it autographed sometime."

A girl *that* excited about Deb's picture book—I might almost have liked her if she hadn't been clinging to Scott's hand again. "Sure, I think Debra would be happy to do that. Fame hasn't affected her at all." I grinned. "Gotta run now. See you. Come on, Beauty, hurry up. Do your business." As I'd hoped, the sight of Beauty squatting, back arched, was a quick exit call for Gwen and Scott. I scooped, and with the serious business over, headed back home with Beauty.

Later, sporting a green jacket that read *Future Guide Dog*, Beauty paced beside me at Gate 6, waiting for Debra's plane. Canine Vision likes foster families to take their dogs everywhere, and airports were a good experience for Beauty.

"Settle down, Beauty. Stay. Sit."

Beauty whimpered as she reluctantly lowered her butt. Dad ran and checked the airport monitor to see that, yes, Flight 404 was really on time and arriving at 17:10—a time he normally spent on the commuter train home from Regal Trust.

Mom held a bouquet of red carnations. She didn't ordinarily go for cut flowers but they were a fundraiser for some women's shelter. She'd swapped the class she usually taught at this hour with another English instructor. All of us waiting, waiting for my big sister.

To me, Debra held all the mysteries of dating in her head—she was practically married after all; I needed her. I

wondered if she still wore black all the time—last Christmas
she had—but now that her book was out, maybe she'd
changed. Then, in the middle of my wondering, I spotted
her; there among a tanned bunch of travelers. She wore
tiny dark-blue sunglasses and, yes, a black long-sleeved shirt
with matching pants. It looked like her mascara had
smeared down her left eye. Not like Debra. Or wasn't that
her, after all?

Debra usually swoops when she walks. She's tall and her
stride is long and confident. Only this girl walked with
smaller, more hesitant steps. I tilted my head. Her jet-black
hair had sprouted bright-red-and-blue streaks, which was
more Debra's style. Was it her or not?

Closer and closer. I squinted. Finally she waved. A small
wave with a small smile; and I ran, Beauty bounding beside
me.

"Debra!" I called with my arms outstretched. As I
reached her I jumped to bear-hug her, knocking down
those tiny blue sunglasses.

That's when I realized that the dark color smudged
down her left cheekbone wasn't mascara at all. Everything
inside me slid around all topsy-turvy, and I felt slightly sick.
My sister's left eye was circled by a deep purple bruise.

Kyle

The Last Perfect Image

Sunset at Waikiki Beach, a pink and golden moment full of soft breezes. *I will never get up on this thing*, I thought as I lay on my surfboard, the sinking sun warm on my back, a curly phone-type cord attached to my ankle. I'd spent three weeks in Hawaii, paid all this month's allowance on the lesson and surfboard rental my final day, and it was going to end like this.

Not that it was a bad way. I mean, I'm not a big athlete. Just holding onto the board—feeling the swells of the ocean lift and drop it—soothed and relaxed me. But it seemed like the whole world stood along the beach, watching, cameras poised. It's the daily event at Waikiki, everyone lining up in front of the pastel-colored hotel towers, all waiting to capture forever the perfect sunset. So much anticipation and expectation. Like all the tourists need one special chance to put pink and gold into their ordinary lives.

Suddenly, I knew something bigger had to happen for me, too. I glanced back at the sun—it was melting like a round pat of butter on an ocean of toast. So surreal.

But then I saw the wave coming. As it rolled toward me, it gathered height and power. Something gathered inside me, too. An urge, a strength, a force. I paddled desperately, gaining on the wave just enough so I could hoist myself off my chest. Then carefully, first onto one

foot and then the second, I straightened slightly, my
ankles and knees bent, my arms unfolding straight out
like wings. The wave connected, the whole surfboard
surging forward. I could feel the power beneath my feet.
I shifted my weight to the left a little to adjust my balance, and then quickly to the right. I felt in control, and
yet not—somehow comfortable with the wildness of that
water, my feet planted securely on top of the board. It
was as if I was in balance with life even as it hurtled me
forward to unknown destinations.

It's a feeling I'd give anything to have back.

All the cameras on the beach flashed, and even
though the real subject of the photos was the sun, I felt
like a star.

And then the sun set, taking my sight with it forever.

OK, it wasn't as dramatic as all that. On the plane
home from Grandma's, my eyes began to fuzz up. I'd
blink and blink but I still couldn't sharpen my focus. I
couldn't watch the movie; it was too annoying. I just kept
wanting to adjust some button to make the picture clear-
er. I headed back for the bathroom, kit in hand, to test
my blood sugar. Maybe I needed more insulin. I pricked
my finger and stuck the blood droplet on the test paper.
I did feel tired, but then who wouldn't on a ten-hour
flight? And I was pretty good about ignoring my symp-
toms. In fact, visiting Grandma in Honolulu had been
about Grandma showing me how to live well and keep
good control of my blood-sugar levels. But Grandma

complained along with me. "Too much compromise, too little hot fudge," she'd say.

Anyway, squished up inside that airline stall I tested a perfectly fine seven on the Glucometer. Especially considering that the last meal I'd had was regulation air fare: little squares of unidentifiable protein, and carbo-hydrate with tomato sauce. I gave myself a shot of four units of insulin and everything should have been fine.

When I landed back at Pearson and stumbled toward Mom she immediately dialed Dr. Worden on her cell. He sent us to an eye specialist who peered into my eyes and grumbled out the word *retinopathy*.

"The blood vessels in your eyes are weakening," he said as he shuffled through his drawer. Then he wrote something on his notepad. He never even looked up.

"But I'm fifteen years old. It's not like they've had a lot of wear and tear," I argued.

"This condition occurs in twenty-five percent of diabetes patients. But you're right, rarely in someone as young as yourself." He tore off the top sheet of his notepad and handed it to Mom. "Still, we'll make an appointment to have the vessels cauterized by laser, and your vision should be fine. Try not to worry."

Up until that moment, I hadn't worried at all. Still, how bad could it be? It was the "*should be fine*" that started things racing inside me. By the time I left the office I needed a candy, I felt so light and faint.

I used to look forward to weekends but then they

scheduled my laser appointments for Friday afternoons.
Two months of ruined weekends. By Thursday my stomach would tighten and I'd have trouble sleeping. Friday
morning I found it hard to swallow my artificially sweetened cereal. On the way to the surgeon's office my knees
would shake, and they'd buckle under me as I collapsed
into the chair. If only I didn't need to stay awake for the
whole procedure. I had to hold perfectly still as the laser
click-clicked, frying each vein closed. Hundreds in every
session. I'd feel queasy at the burnt-hair smell of lasered
tissue, even though the nurse swore it was only the smell
of the gases combining. Acidy-sweet cereal bits backed
up my throat. Afterward it was as though mallets pounded against the back of my eyes, so Saturday was another
ruined day.

I began to peer at the world through a sheet of
waxed paper, watching blurry shapes move around. Next,
the specialist recommended surgery to remove the blood
and scar tissue, one eye at a time, with a space of a couple of weeks in between. At least for those I was put out.
I didn't think I could stand being awake as the doctor
popped out my eyeball and cut slits in the back of it to
relieve the pressure.

Each time, I'd awaken with horrible headaches.
Those surgeries worked well; at least the wax paper
opened up in the middle for a time. But then a black
dot would form, and then another.

And over ten months the next two surgeries worked

well, too, until one dot turned into a hole that swallowed up my central vision. I had to look at the world sideways through the wax paper curtains on my eyes. The next surgery didn't work at all. My left retina had detached and that eye saw nothing.

"Do I have to go through it again? What if this one doesn't work either?" I asked the specialist, turning so I could at least see the outline of his face through the wax curtain of my right eye.

"Don't you think we have to take the chance?"

Only I have to take the chance, I thought, but I nodded.

Before the final surgery, I prayed and prayed for a permanent solution. I just knew I couldn't take any more operations. And when the doctor removed the bandages in the recovery room, it was a miracle. I could see my fingernails, the hair on the back of my hand— more detail than I'd seen in months.

He rewrapped the bandages around my head. "Keep absolutely still. We don't want any complications." I lay there the whole day, hardly daring to breath, let alone move a muscle.

That night I got my prayer answered. When the doctor removed the bandages a second time, my world had been swallowed up by darkness. I could see no more. My second retina had detached. I had my permanent solution.

CHAPTER 2

Disasters

"Don't make a fuss, Mother, really. It was the stupidest of accidents," Debra said as she brushed Mom's hand away from her bruised cheek. "Imagine. I was bending over to put on my boots and just at that precise moment, Rolph came home." She shrugged her shoulders. "Boof! The doorknob hit my cheek. It didn't hurt nearly as badly as it looks."

"He should be more careful when he opens the door," Dad grumbled.

"Oh, definitely. Rolph feels awful about it. He can't stop apologizing." Debra smiled brightly as she inhaled the scent of her flowers and changed the subject. "I love carnations, Mom. Thank you."

Does Debra even bend over to put her boots on? I wondered. At our house she sat on a chair in the living room. Mom complained about that a lot. I stared at Deb's bruise again and winced. *He better not have hit her*, I thought.

Beauty's tail slapped my leg. "Good girl. Don't worry." I stooped down a little to pat her. "We're leaving now."

Dad grabbed Debra's luggage cart, which was piled high with suitcases, duffel bags and a huge portfolio case. "You sure packed enough for two weeks." Dad sounded gruff but his smile widened as he pushed the cart into the elevator.

"Did you buy a lot of cool stuff on Rodeo Drive?" I asked as we all squeezed in around the cart. The elevator lurched down.

"Not for me, I didn't. Too *bourgeois*." She touched my nose with her finger. "But I did find an outfit for you, little sister." I remembered how I used to hate when she called me that or treated me that way. Now I wanted to soak it all in. I'd missed Debra so much.

It took an hour to get home in the heavy traffic and the moment our van pulled in the driveway, I leapt out with Beauty. All that waiting had made me tense and I needed to move around, just like the dog. So I ran around the yard, with Beauty barking and chasing at my heels. It felt great, like a celebration that Debra was home.

"Can you help with the bags first, Elizabeth?" Dad called. He did look pretty weighed down so we ran back to the car.

I hung Deb's carry-on around Beauty's neck and reached for her portfolio, only Debra insisted on carrying that herself. So I took a duffel bag in each hand and raced Beauty into the house and up the stairs to Deb's room.

"Maybe Deb needs to lie down and rest first. Or maybe

she'd like some privacy to unpack," Mom called up after us.

"That's perfectly all right," she told Mom.

I took the bag off Beauty and we both jumped onto her bed, sprawled over it, waiting. Waiting for all the answers Debra could give me.

"Goodness," Debra said as she stepped into the room. "I'd almost forgotten what it was like to live in the animal kingdom." She sank down beside Beauty, stroking her glossy brown head. "Hello, beautiful doggie." We sat together like that for a while, with only the sound of Beauty lapping at Debra's hands. My dog, my sister and me. For a moment I forgot all my questions.

Then Debra unzipped her portfolio.

"Wow, what's that?" I asked.

"*Camel on a Surfboard*. You know, the sequel to the first book I illustrated." She frowned as she placed the picture on her drawing desk. "Except there's something not right about it."

Hmm. This camel *did* look a little off. "Maybe the eyes…no, the mouth…the face."

"The legs, the body, I know…I just can't capture that same playful mood I had in *Camel on a Skateboard*." Debra tilted her head to see another angle and I noticed all the broken red veins in her bruised eye.

"Maybe you should relax and unwind before you think about fixing up a painting," I told her.

She pursed her mouth and squinted. "Mmm." Then she spun around and forced a smile. "Probably I should show you your present," she said.

Beauty wagged and seemed excited. Always the fashion-conscious Lab.

Debra unlocked her large suitcase and scooped out a beautiful gray bag with the fuchsia letters *Rodeo* across it. "Here." She handed it to me.

I quickly pulled out a crisp cherry-colored sundress with tiny spaghetti straps. "Oh, gosh, it's beautiful. Do you think I could wear it my first day to high school? I'm so nervous. I just want everything to go perfectly."

"Sure. Take off your T-shirt and slip it on over." She helped me pull my top over my head and held the dress above me as I shrugged into it.

"Now look in the mirror." Debra pushed my shoulders so that I faced the mirror hanging from her door.

I liked how the cherry color refused to back down from the orangy color of my hair. I also liked the idea that the dress was just a little unusual for me. If I should bump into Scott, he would have to take notice of me.

"Debra, do you think there's only one person in the whole world who we're destined to be with? You know, like Dad and Mom, or"—I forced myself to add—"like you and Rolph?" I wanted to talk to her about how my best friend Alicia could just "fall in like" with so many different guys and how I just kept wanting Scott back. And how humiliating that felt, when he was so over me.

Debra turned and stared at her painting again, smile dissolving.

"Deb?" I called her gently.

"I'm not really up to leading the lonely hearts club,
Liz." She spun around to face me. "No one else knows this
yet, but I've left Rolph." Her words snapped at me like
something brittle cracking in half. Then she blew out a big
sigh.

I wanted to be happy. I had my sister back all to myself.
Only she looked so sad. I reached to her, but she pulled
away, and I saw a tear slide down her cheek.

"If you'll excuse me, I'd like to be alone now."

My stomach clenched into a tight fist. I looked at that
bruise—he couldn't have done that, could he? Maybe she
was better off without him. I knew I would be.

I swallowed hard before talking. "OK," I finally said.

"Thanks for the dress. C'mon, Beauty."

I needed to get out of there—to smash something, to
run hard, to scream. It was the only way I could lose the
tight feeling inside. Or maybe there was one other way. I
stopped halfway down the hall.

"Beauty, do you want to go Rollerblading?" I asked.

Beauty's whole body shimmied with delight and she
jumped up on my leg. *Is it true? Can we really go, can we go now?*
Her eyes asked. They were a golden amber color, much
lighter than our first foster puppy's—she'd been a black
Lab. Somehow Beauty II's eyes seemed even more human.

"Well, let's go then," I said softly. I quickly changed out
of my new dress while she nosed through a pile of dirty
clothes to find my wrist guards.

"Good stuff," I told her outside on the steps, when she dropped them in my lap. Sometimes it really did seem she'd make a great guide dog. I gave her an extra hard hug, which is what I'd really wanted to do with Debra. Then I pulled away so I could get my skates on.

"She's left Rolph, Beauty. That has to be good, don't you think?"

Beauty wagged and wiggled. She seemed even more excited about that news than I was, as she loped off beside me, a big dog grin across her face. The sidewalk rumbled beneath my skates as we traveled up to our favorite park where only a couple of days ago the pavers had been working.

"Let's check out the new path, Beauty!" I turned into the park and couldn't believe my eyes. There's nothing quite as great as fresh, smooth blacktop to Rollerblade on. The rumbling turned into a smoother murmur as my wheels glided across the new surface. "Aw, yeah, it's definitely our day, girl. Rolph's gone. The whole trail is paved!"

Past the swings and slides, past the monkey bars and teeter-totter, through the forest, toward a hill.

Stupid Rolph. Stupid Rolph, my wheels echoed. He'd always been a bit of a bully, if you asked me. *Stop thinking about him*! I willed myself.

I needed to bend my knees and really push hard to climb that incline. My calves burned by the time we stopped at the top. I breathed in and looked over the park, seeing clearly. Scott would have loved this path. We used to always

Rollerblade together.

Debra will know how to get Scott back. Now that she's back for good, she can tell me exactly how to act and talk. Never mind Rolph—this would all turn out OK, at least for me.

"Whoa! Look how far down the path goes, Beauty. Do we chance it?" The trouble with it being a new trail was that I didn't know, and couldn't see from here, whether the incline ended in a big curve. When you pick up that much speed, it's sometimes impossible to make a turn.

Beauty sat down while I squinted at the path some more. Finally I turned and patted her head. What was the point of working so hard to get to the top of the hill if you didn't treat yourself to the thrill of skating down? She licked at my hand.

"You know what, girl? It's been a perfect day so far. I say I go for it."

Beauty looked at me. *Are you sure you know what you're doing?* her golden eyes asked. But that's the best thing about dogs: they don't lecture and nag you like a parent. "You stay here, just in case I wipe out."

Finally, Beauty seemed to nod, dropped down and opened her mouth into a relaxed pant.

"Stay!" I reminded her, holding up one finger. And I knew she would. I'd trained her by making her wait for her food every day, counting to ten before I said go. I positioned myself away from her, spread my feet apart, bent my knees and crouched down. Slowly, I pushed off.

But of course, I gathered speed immediately. Faster and still faster. The wind rushed up against my face and through my hair. Life couldn't get any better.

"Woo-hoo!" I hollered. *"Rolph's gone!"*

The park around me turned into a green blur. I couldn't even breathe. And then I spotted Little Stone Bridge partly hidden by a bush. No curve in the path, but there it lay—something even worse. Like a mouth full of metal teeth, a sewer grate grinned across the entire path.

The only other time I nearly killed myself while Rollerblading was on a sewer grate. That was with the first Beauty, and then I hadn't even been skating as fast as today.

What could I do? What could I do?

I hurtled faster and faster toward those teeth. There was only one thing I could think of. I jumped from the pavement and threw myself to the grass.

Kyle

The Date

On my sixteenth birthday, I had the perfect date planned with Maddie. Well, it could have been perfect if I'd have gotten my driver's license instead of going blind.

But at least I still had a girlfriend. Maddie had even come to visit me in the hospital from time to time. If you're going to have to live in constant darkness, it'll be at least bearable if there's someone to share it with you.

Share is probably the wrong word. The ironic thing
was that I'd been afraid of the dark all my life, and Mom
had put a different kind of night-light in my Christmas
stocking every year to help me cope. When everything
stayed dark, Madison was the night-light I pictured to
keep the fear away.

Maddie and I held hands in the back and I imagined
Mom's eyes on us through the rear-view mirror. I wondered what I looked like. Not only was Mom in charge of
driving, but she was also my wardrobe consultant.

My blue socks and blue jeans were coded with two
beads, just as the rehab teacher from the Institute had
shown me. My white socks and khaki pants were one
bead. All of my shirts pretty much went with either; still,
four beads meant the tops were bright colors, three
beads meant they were dark. Three beads on pants stood
for black.

Mom told me that it looked like a sunny day—why
didn't I go for a brighter look? I'd dressed up in a
three-beaded combo that Saturday, for my first date
since the final surgery. I couldn't change. Blind or not,
your mom can't run your life. Still, I had to let her give
me the once-over and I felt like kicking myself when she
told me I was wearing mismatched sneakers. They did
feel different, now that she'd mentioned it. Why hadn't I
noticed on my own? And when would I learn to keep
them together?

Was there anything Mom had missed? I couldn't

help wondering as I held Madison's hand. I loved the way it felt, the top of her hand smooth and cool, the palm soft and slightly warmer, but not damp like mine.

I imagined Maddie's face. She had wide, surprised green eyes with heavy brown eyebrows that rose up and down to comment on things. Up: "Oh really?" Down: "Don't be silly!" Then she'd chuckle or smile at things I said.

Her pale white skin sunburned too easily, so she'd wear the most bizarre hats to protect it. I loved those hats. But I loved her upturned nose the best. No hat could protect it as it freckled, just a little, in the spring.

I'd known her since kindergarten and probably loved her since then, too. Still, it took me years to work up the courage to kiss the tip of Maddie's sun-sprinkled nose and ask her out. That had been at the beginning of the summer, just before the black hole had opened up in the middle of my vision. But now that the hole had swallowed up everything, if I aimed for her nose, I might kiss her square on the eyeball—and wouldn't her brows jump up high then?

I wanted to kiss her in the back of the car that sunny Saturday afternoon, but I was wearing sunglasses. Mom said they made me look like a movie star but really they hid what Maddie had liked best about me, my eyes. She said they were the friendliest blue, like faded jeans—especially when I smiled and the skin alongside them crinkled up.

Now my eyes wouldn't focus or smile for her. In
fact, my eyeballs were actually shrinking. "Don't be
ridiculous," my father drawled in his heaviest Southern
accent when I first asked him if he'd noticed. But he uses
his accent when he most needs to convince.

"Hardly at all," Mom answered, and she tousled my
hair like a kid. The hair tousling showed she was lying
too.

"Maybe just a bit," my little sister Shawna agreed,
and the tone of her voice sounded so sad, I hugged her
and wiped the wetness from her cheek. Lately when I
stuck my finger against an eye, I could feel the gap
between it and the lid.

So do you take your sunglasses off to kiss the girl you
have known forever and been seeing officially for five
months (and not seeing—at least not clearly—for the last
two)?

The wind from my mother's open window blew
against my face. The smell of fall-leaf bonfire mingled
with Maddie's tangerine perfume. Sunrise, it was called.
I squeezed her hand and she squeezed back. Could I
even chance kissing her at all? The radio played a really
dumb golden oldie, something about leaving a cake out
in the rain. My mother sang along. I took a deep breath.
What the hey! I'd keep the glasses on.

I leaned forward and reached for her chin with my
hand. Good, I touched it first try. Then I held it as my
head moved forward. If my lips missed, they would con-

26

nect with her chin or maybe even her nose. That would-
n't be so bad either.

But as my face moved closer and closer, my lips did
land perfectly, soft, soft, against hers. And she kissed
back. I knew for that one moment she still liked me.
Who cared about driving anymore? The world would be
an almost perfect place as long as Maddie still wanted to
kiss me back.

I heard her contented sigh. It took me forever to
force myself to pull away again. But Mom was giving us a
little cough as the car rolled up to our favorite fast-food
restaurant, Poutine Palace.

I'm not sure how awkward I looked, scrambling out
after Maddie, but I think I did OK, walking along beside
her, holding her hand.

"It's such a nice day. Let's eat at the picnic table,"
Maddie suggested.

We ordered the house specialty from the takeout
window. French fries heaped with hot brown gravy and
melting white cheese. It meant a four-dose shot of
insulin before lunch and plain salad that night. But it
would be worth it.

Slipping my knees around the bench part of the
table, first one then the other, took an extra bit of wan-
gling. I felt the table shift as Madison sat down across
from me.

We always use a wooden fork to stab those fries and
shovel them into our mouths. So I started. Delicious—

gooey, spicy and smooth.

The fries were long and I kept wiping the corners of my mouth and chin so that the hot cheese wouldn't burn me or make me look like an exploding zit.

That's when it happened. Maybe I'd gotten overconfident and too quick. Maybe it was the distraction of the seagulls screaming for us to throw them something. In any case, I felt the end of one fry slide right up my nostril.

Is there any way you can calmly and coolly yank a scalding, cheesy piece of potato from your nose? "Ow, crap!" I jumped up, banging my knees. I pulled out the fry and swiped at my nose with some crumpled napkins. My shrinking eyes watered from behind their glasses.

"Poor baby," Maddie said as she kissed my nose, for a change. Maddie could still turn even the worst moment into something special and fun.

Or the most special and fun moment into the worst.

After we finished eating, we walked together to the park.

"Exercise will bring my blood sugar back in line," was my excuse, but I knew we wouldn't work up too much of a sweat.

We strolled past the playground. I heard kids squealing and yelling from the swings and slides. We continued past the monkey bars and teeter-totter; I knew there was a bench nearby but Maddie wanted to keep walking. Through the forest, up a hill and down near Little Stone Bridge, judging by the sound of the water nearby.

"Hey, you're taking this exercise thing too seriously," I told her.

Finally we sat down on a large, flat rock near the brook, which gurgled over some rocks. I swung my arm around Maddie and we just relaxed, listening to the world around us. That was all good too. Then I wanted to tell her how much she meant to me. "You know, without you, I don't think I could stand my life."

"Don't say that," she whispered. Embarrassed? Shy? I couldn't understand the tone of her voice, so I simply leaned toward her to kiss her again. She moved away and cleared her throat. "Kyle, I'm sorry...I just can't do this anymore. I know it's your birthday, but I have something I really need to tell you... And I don't want you to think this is about you going blind.... "

That's when I finally clued in to why she had to walk so far and hard. It was like someone had stabbed a scalding hot French fry into my heart.

"You were always in the hospital and I, well, I'll never stop loving you...."

At that moment, I inhaled so sharply I began choking on the dry air.

"...But I only love you as a friend."

"Stop," I gasped between coughs. "Madison, stop." I turned toward her. "Don't!" I said, as she brushed my cheek with her hand.

The last thing I wanted was Maddie's pity. I breathed in more slowly and let the breath out shakily. "Could you do me one favor?" I whispered.

"What, Kyle?"

"Could you just get up and go?"

"Kyle?"

"Please. I have my cell phone."

"But do you know where you are?"

I nodded and felt her brush away from me.

"See you at school, then?" she pleaded.

Well, you'll *see* me, I thought bitterly. But I didn't trust my voice to say anything more.

"Good-bye, Kyle."

I waved her away. I couldn't watch her hips sway or her hair bounce on her shoulders. I couldn't catch glimpses of her walking away even from the sides of my eyes, the way I used to do before the last surgery. I would never see Maddie again.

Out there in the world of bright light and happiness, a gentle breeze rustled the leaves. From the top of the hill I heard a dog barking and then a girl's laughter ringing like bells. The laughter turned into shouts of exhilaration that seemed to be coming closer. Such joy— had I ever felt that?

I swallowed hard and squeezed what was left of my eyes hard together. For a moment I flashed back to my last sunset at Waikiki. *Never, ever again*, I thought. I felt like yelling and crying, but who knew where Maddie was? I didn't want her to catch me.

Then suddenly I heard a muffled thump and a cry of pain. "Ohh! Ouch! Owww!"

Yes, that's how I feel. Was I imagining it?

Now I heard a girl crying softly somewhere near the path. She sounded like she was in physical pain. I wanted her to keep crying, to cry for me. I loved her quiet sobbing. It was the most beautiful sound in the world at that moment.

"Are you all right?" I tried to call. But it came out in a hoarse whisper. And then I heard loud barking. A dog panted hot and smelly breath into my face. *RAWF!* I pushed a wet muzzle away from me, nervously, hoping the dog's teeth wouldn't sink into my hand.

"Go away. Go get someone else. I can't even help myself."

CHAPTER 3

Elizabeth and Beauty

The First Day of High School

Every part of my body hurt—I could barely sit up. I felt so angry with myself. Geez, why hadn't I just kept skating across that grate? Could anything worse have happened? I started crying, not only because everything throbbed and ached but also because I was angry. And I hate crying, which made me angrier and made me cry more.

"Beauty, I thought I told you to stay!" I yelled when I saw her galloping to some guy in sunglasses sitting on the rock. All dressed in black, with those dark glasses and glossy black gelled hair, the guy looked cool and mysterious, like a fashion model or a secret agent. He seemed to be watching me, too, and totally put off by Beauty, pushing her away. Being such a blubbering mess, I was glad when my stupid dog finally came back to me.

Ignoring the stranger, I took off my Rollerblades and placed my hands on Beauty's back to brace myself as I got up. Then I limped home, Beauty brushing against me all the way.

When we finally made it through the door, Mom and Debra were having tea together and didn't notice us coming in. I'd forgotten that part about having Deb live at home. Her life always took up my parents' whole attention span. There would be nothing left for me. The bad side of having my sister back.

Then Mom yelled at me about my dirty socks. Maybe not having their attention was a good thing after all. I'd soak them in bleach, I promised her to get her off my back.

Then I ran a bath and crated Beauty, knowing from experience that she might join me, otherwise. As I soaked in the hot water I watched my bruises color in. How could I wear my new dress tomorrow—let alone walk? Not a great start to high school.

But I didn't have to worry. Next morning, Debra was up for hair and wardrobe consultation. "God, you bruise as easily as I do," she said, staring at my legs. "Never mind. I'm a pro at hiding it all with makeup."

She sipped from her cappuccino as she considered my hair next. "Why don't we work *with* your natural curl instead of against it? We can scrunch it up with some hair gel, and maybe even coax some ringlets in." Debra ripped off a bit of croissant with her fingers. Beauty leapt up, eyeing her, ears slightly raised. Ripped-off bits usually meant doggy treats for her. "It's amazingly quick and easy," Debra continued, popping the croissant corner in her mouth. Beauty's ears sank, along with her body and hopes.

"Sounds great," I said, slurping up the last bit of milk from my cereal.

Then I filled Beauty's dish with dog food. "Come on,
Beauty. One Mississauga, two Mississauga, three…" I whispered under my breath, holding a finger in front of her as she
sat patiently. At ten I told her, "OK, girl, go!" Beauty leapt
forward and annihilated her food, crunching happily. I headed for the shower.

Afterwards, back in her room, Debra performed her
magic. My hair looked glossy wet, in smooth curls instead of
sproings. Perfect. She blended concealer and foundation over
the bruises on my legs so that they disappeared entirely. "Take
my sandals," she suggested, rummaging out some cork plat-
form shoes for me.

I slipped into them. Only one wide navy strap at the front
wrapped across the top of my foot. When I walked, it felt as
though I might slip out. My toes clung tightly.

Debra clucked when I stepped in front of her full-length
mirror. "With the short dress and big soles your legs go on
forever. You'll have Scotty panting." Debra smiled.

"What makes you think…"

She waved her hand. In a whiny little-girl voice she mim-
icked me: "'Do you think there's only one person in the whole
world you're destined to be with?'"

"He goes out with someone else, though," I told her.

"That's too bad." She wagged a finger at me and spoke in
her older, wiser voice. "Still, in high school you'll meet many
more interesting men." She winked. "Especially if you dress
like that."

"But I only ever like Scott."

"Well, then don't give up so easily. What's the one thing he admires most about you?" she asked.

"I don't know. Can you take Beauty for a walk today?" The word walk, as softly as I'd said it, must have sent secret vibrations to Beauty. She bounded up the stairs and instantly appeared at our feet, wagging her tail frantically.

"Beauty!" she snapped her fingers. "That's what always brings him back to you. You're right," Debra said.

I felt confused. "Honestly, Debra, I think his girlfriend Gwen is a lot prettier than I am."

"No. I don't mean your beauty. This Beauty." She pointed to the dog, who went wild with joy over the attention. "With her guide-dog jacket on, can't you take her everywhere?" She had to shove Beauty down now, the dog was so excited.

"You want me to take her to my first day at high school?"

"Yes, yes," she said too eagerly. The dog jumped on Deb again.

"Phooey, Beauty!" I scolded her. It's the word trainers recommend. Dogs don't like the sound, for some reason.

"Don't take this the wrong way," Debra continued, "but sometimes you're just a little standoffish with people." Deb patted Beauty as she spoke, to calm her down. "And this way, everyone will talk to you. Besides, Scotty Dog has always seemed enamored with the way you raise these animals."

She made a lot of sense, and for sure Debra didn't want to look after Beauty that day. So I snapped on her future-guide-dog coat and together we headed off to Alicia's house.

Gripping my toes to my shoes and limping all the way, I

took a lot longer than I should have. Alicia already stood waiting outside.

"Hey, Beauty!" she hollered, waving to the dog. "You coming to school today too?" Beauty strained to reach her. "Good idea, Elizabeth. Dogs are great conversation starters." She patted Beauty's head. "You look great, by the way. I love the hair, the dress, even the sandals...."

Just then one of my shoes sailed ahead of my foot. My instep banged down on the hard edge of the back. "Ow, drat. Geez, it's hard work to look good."

"You just have to get used to walking in heels, that's all," Alicia said.

When we got to the school, we had to find and report to our homerooms. This all took longer than it should have, because Beauty made friends with everyone along the way. I thought the custodian might be upset by an animal in her school, but she just cooed at Beauty. When Beauty barked her hello, the school secretary peeked her head out of the office and then squeezed through the crowd of students around us to pat her.

So where's Scott? I thought. He seemed like the only person we weren't attracting. We finally stepped into homeroom and the teacher spoke directly with Beauty instead of me. "Well, hello. Aren't you the good, good dog? Everyone else is lined up outside. Do you want to join them, eh, doggie? Do you?" Beauty wagged her understanding and agreement, then dragged me back out.

"Hi, Beauty," another voice called out. I saw that it was our tour guide—Scott's girlfriend, Gwen. Hmm. Seniors led tours, and Scott was only in second year, so that meant he was seeing an older woman.

I gritted my teeth as the line moved forward. More walking, more toe gripping. I could feel blisters forming on the bottom of both big toes. Beauty strained ahead, following Gwen and whipping me with her tail.

"This is the office, where you go for your late slips. They call home if you're away, so despite what you've heard about kids skipping, you do get caught," Gwen warned us. She showed us the library, which was ten times the size of the library back at my old school, not even including the computer lab attached to it. Next came the family studies room, the chemistry class, the biology lab, the music room and the technical studies workroom. So many rooms, for so many courses we didn't even have in elementary school.

"I'm never going to find my way around here," I told Alicia as we walked.

"Well, don't worry about it," Gwen answered. "People are happy to help. Now, Mrs. Johnson, the principal, is waiting in Gym 3 for you."

Several groups of first-year students joined us as we filed into one of the five huge gyms. Then Mrs. Johnson lectured us about the high-school student's most important tool to success. She waved a day planner.

"Nobody will spoon-feed you. High school is hard work and you need to keep on track." She warned against skipping classes and she encouraged us to participate. Then she finished with, "These are the best days of your lives."

We shuffled out of Gym 3 just as the first-period bell rang.

Somehow a group of guys wedged in between me and the group, and I felt as though I were caught in some strange male undertow.

One of the guys whistled at me. Was he making fun of me? I wasn't sure, but I straightened and walked more forcefully against the current.

"Tweenie babies—my favorite," a second one said.

"Excuse me," I said softly as I tried squeezing through them to get back to my group, my face flaming. "Excuse me!" I repeated. Beauty growled, and finally I was able to barrel through. Just as I made it, though, my right sandal hurtled half the hall ahead of me.

"I got it!" a familiar voice called. But the guy who scooped up the sandal started running away. Yeah, sure, people were all helpful around here.

Beauty barked. No way would she let anyone get away with that. I tore off my other sandal as she bolted forward. Then I flew like some kind of human kite behind her. Down one hall, around a corner, down a flight of stairs...Would I ever remember my way back? The guy ducked into a huge room that turned out to be the cafeteria. But how would I ever find him there?

I took a deep breath. Even at ten-thirty in the morning, the lunchroom smell hit me. Onions, gravy and pizza, all mixed in together. Most of the metal tables had students sitting around them. How could they be hungry already?

I rubbed at my bruised hip for a moment. I'd have to give up on that sandal. Debra would be so peeved at me, but worse, I'd have to spend the rest of the day in bare feet. How impressive would that be? And these were the best days of my life? Arrr.

Then Beauty yanked forward again, leading and guiding me to...oh my gosh, it was Scott.

He slumped at a table, dark sunglasses hiding his eyes, the hood of his school sweatshirt covering his head. I would never have recognized him—except for Beauty's wild reaction to him and the two French fries hanging from his nose. Who else would shove fast food up their nose?

Beauty leapt onto him and ate the French fries from his nostrils. I started to laugh and I wanted to cry. Should I kiss him or kill him? There, on the table in front of him, sat my other sandal.

Kyle

Back to School

There are two different canes blind people can carry. They both work in exactly the same way, but one is white and large and used to tap, tap your way around: a mobility cane. The second is white and tent-pole collapsible so that you can hide it away when you don't need it. It's supposed to identify you as visually handicapped: an identi-cane. But I didn't want to be identified. Still, I had to practice a few

days a week with a rehab worker to learn how to use either.
He helped me get my bearings in the school halls by guiding me around on the weekend. The first morning back at
school, however, I collapsed the identi-cane, tucking it into
my backpack.

"You know, you've spent so much energy hiding your
diabetes. Are you going to try to hide your blindness now?"
my mom asked.

"Hide it?" I slipped down my sunglasses. "Who are you
trying to kid?"

But she was right. A vivid picture snapped into my
mind: me shooting up with insulin in an ensuite bathroom
at Maddie's, surprised halfway through by her mom. Her
eyebrows—which Maddie had inherited—jumped up and
joined together in a look of horror. Then she backed up
and I had to chase after her later to answer the question she
wouldn't ask. After all, it's too rude to say, "Hey, are you a
heroin addict?"

You could tell she wasn't happy. Every boyfriend's a
potential husband, Maddie explained. She wouldn't want a
drug addict for her daughter's future mate. And I could tell
by looking at her mom's face, as I explained about my diabetes, that she wouldn't want someone suffering from an
incurable disease as a potential father to her grandchild,
either. What would her eyebrows have done if she'd seen
me with a white cane?

If I could just hide my blindness for a few extra heart-
beats, maybe people would give me a chance to be a real

person, instead of a poster boy for a handicap.

Mom drove me to school early. "I wish you had called one of your friends to meet you, at least on the first day," she told me, grabbing my hand before I could take off.

One of my friends. Trouble was that "one of my friends" was my only friend. When a guy isn't a big athlete, he doesn't necessarily collect a ton of male buddies. I chummed around with some people from Band way back last year, and then everybody pretty much fell away when I went out with Maddie.

Music and Maddie, my only friends. Here it was my first day back at school, everyone else's second week. I squeezed Mom's hand back, just to duck the kiss that the tone in her voice warned me about. Then I made a big show of bringing out the identi-cane to tap my way into the building.

Once inside though, I quickly folded it away, shuffling along the hall, running my hand across the lockers to find my way. Not bad—this was working, I could handle this. First room, second room, hallway, turn. I'd counted and planned this all out with Jack, my Orientation and Mobility instructor.

And then the bell rang. Three hundred kids crowded into the school, all of them, it seemed, crashing into me on their way by. I lost track of when I had turned left and how many doors I had passed. Two days of practicing with Jack, all of the labeling and memory tricks he'd shown me, blanked out of my head in one hot sweaty moment. I'd told

him this would never work. Still I'd hoped. I could be normal; I could fit in. I wanted to whip out my cane and fling
it at the mass of sighted bodies. To snap it across one of
their backs or against a locker.

Someone grabbed me by the elbow. I smelled tangerine. I felt a light switch on inside me, felt warm and bright.

"Come on, let me help. That's what friends do,"
Maddie told me. "And you're in my first-period history
class. It only makes sense that I take you there." She just
dragged me along.

Wish I could have yanked my arm away and yelled, *I
don't want you as a friend! I can do this myself!* But I couldn't. I didn't
even want to stop at my locker and risk losing her help.
"Could you slow down a little?" I asked as we turned down
the hall.

"Um, sure." She slowed to turtle speed. "You know,
there's a new girl who brought her dog to school first day."

"That shouldn't be allowed."

"Oh, right. I forgot about your thing with dogs." We
turned into the classroom. "Point is it's a future guide dog.
You should check that out."

I *don't have a* thing *with dogs*, I wanted to say as I fingered
the scar on my cheek. Maddie pushed me toward a chair. As
I sat down, I quickly slipped my tape recorder into the desk.
When Mr. Fulmer spoke, I would press the first button,
Record. I'd started note-taking like this last year. It sucked.

I slumped into the chair, trying to look casual. My
sunglasses slipped down. Stupid things. I pushed them back

up. Chairs scraped across the floor to the left and to the right. I heard Mr. Fulmer clear his throat from the front. "Yes, Ryan?"

Ryan—some kid I didn't know or remember. "Sir, when's that blind guy going to get here?"

Mr. Fulmer had warned them? I squirmed for a moment in the big hush that followed. Most of the kids must have known anyway. They'd likely heard some rumor about what had happened, even if they didn't miss the quiet guy from Band.

But Ryan hadn't recognized me as the blind guy and that made me feel strangely proud, as though I'd achieved something. Kids wear dark glasses inside all the time. Without the cane, who could know for sure? Maybe this would be OK; maybe I could be myself.

"Ryan? Four seats in back of you is 'the blind guy'," Mr. Fulmer said, emphasizing the last two words. "Say hello, Kyle."

I silently waved my hand just above my head.

"Don't you feel like pulling your feet from your mouth now, Ryan?" Kids sputtered and tittered over that one. And then Mr. Fulmer continued with his lesson, not allowing any awkwardness to take over the class.

I relaxed and listened to the discussion on the causes of the First World War.

Tonight I would have to replay the whole thing on tape, instead of just skimming some handwritten notes. Then I would scan the reading assignment onto disk and get my

computer to read my homework for me. I'd choose Psycho
Eddie's voice—a rasping, breathy read that would make every
fact sound like a whispered secret. Maybe I wouldn't fall
asleep then, the way I often did listening to talking books.

When the bell rang, I only had to hang back a little and
Maddie scooped me up by my elbow again. French class
turned out to be likewise, a breeze. For me, other languages
were like music, something I picked up really easily. I wondered if there was a Psycho Pierre voice on my program.

"Do you wanna come to lunch at the mall?" Maddie
asked after English class. "Not just with me. With a gang of
us?"

Did I want to sit all by myself in the cafeteria, or hang
around with someone I loved much more than a friend?

"The mall, sure," I said. "Let's just throw my backpack
in the locker first."

Too late, I realized that my folded identi-cane had
stayed behind in that locker. *What the hey*, I thought. I heard
about ten giggling voices suddenly surround me. I had
plenty of girls to guide me.

Then some loud, swearing guys joined us—yeah, I recognized Ryan's four-letter dialogue in among the other
ones.

"Hey, you're Kyle, the blind guy. Cool."

It suddenly did seem cool. Another girl looped her
arm in mine. "Hi, it's me, Rebecca," she said, a little loud-
ly. "Do you have a sixth sense? You know, because you're
blind."

"No." Stupid ideas people had about blindness—like there was some gift attached, to make up for the disability. "Even if I did, technically it would only be a fifth sense."

Rebecca chuckled.

But it was a dry, I-don't-really-get-the-joke kind of sound. Not like that laughter I'd heard from the girl in the park—full of energy and happiness.

Feeling like an idiot, I stumbled down a curb, and then tripped up the walk on the other side of the street. But no one said anything. Probably what they expected from The Blind Kid. When we walked into the mall, the floor was smoother; and I thought I did a lot better, really blending in. I ordered a veggie sub in the food court, thinking even a blind boy could eat a sandwich without getting hot things up his nose.

"Here, let me get that sauce off your chin," Maddie said.

Too late to stop her, I felt a napkin brushing at me.

"Hey, Kyle, would you like to feel my face?" a different girl asked. "It's Sarah, beside you. Really, it's OK." Without waiting for an answer, she placed my hands on her cheek. Her skin felt soft and warm. There's just nothing like a girl's skin, anyway. But my hands froze. I didn't really want to run my sweaty palms over her nose and eyes. What would it do, anyway? Did she think I could cut-and-paste an image of her with this touching?

"Heh, heh. Kyle gets to feel Sarah up," Ryan said.

I dropped my hands immediately.

"Hey, I gotta hit the can," he said.

"Me too," I said. "Can you take me?"

He didn't answer really quickly. Too bad I wasn't a girl—they go to the bathroom together in flocks. "Well, OK," he finally said, "just as long as you know I prefer chicks. Heh, heh," he said, grabbing a piece of my shirt and tugging me along. "Meet you at the arcade after," he called to his buddies.

We walked quickly and I heard the door squeak open. "Just point me to the stalls," I said to Ryan, not wanting to trust my aim at the urinals. At least not in front of Ryan.

"Over there." He kind of pushed me into a door, which swung open. I stepped through, fumbled to close it, fumbled to try to lock it and then fumbled with my zipper. Everything took ten times longer with all my nervous fumbling. And then, just as I raised my T-shirt to shoot a few units of insulin into my gut, the door squeaked open again.

"Hey, man, let's go," I heard one of my other lunch pals call. "The new Killer Commando game is in. They're giving away free games to the first twenty people."

"Ah, keep your shirt on. I'm coming," Ryan's voice answered. I heard some more door squeaking and banging. Then nothing.

"Hey! Hey!" I called out as I put my Novapen away. I hoped against hope that Ryan hadn't just taken off. But no one answered. I banged open the stall door and tried again. "Ryan, are you here?"

Nobody answered.

CHAPTER 4

Elizabeth and Beauty

Strange...

Beauty gave Scott's face an appreciative slurp, then studied the fries on the table. I wanted to sock Scott, but he tilted his head, reminding me of the first Beauty, when I caught her chewing up my favorite desert boots. And suddenly I wanted to hug him instead. Only Scott belonged to someone else too, just like Beauty I. So I ended up feeling stupid, like my arms and legs had grown miles too long in the Rodeo Drive sundress. A "mommy longlegs" with dirty, blistered feet.

I made a quick grab for the sandal on the table.

Scott caught my arm and grinned at me. "Don't I get a kiss for finding your shoe?" He leaned toward me. I could feel his breath against my cheek.

"Finding?" The shoe in my hand turned into a weapon. "More like stealing," I said as I swung at him.

He, of course, caught my other arm. "You are under my power," he said in low commando cybertones as he tugged me toward him. "Resistance is futile." Then he puckered his lips into a fish mouth. "Kiss me."

That voice, the hood and sunglasses, a new set of French-fry tusks…I shook my head. Well, he was toying with me, obviously.

But his sunglasses slipped for a moment and I stared into his dark brown eyes. He didn't look away immediately, and there was something there; I knew it. And then, dropping one of my arms, he quickly pushed the glasses back up. Two white dots appeared on his cheeks. With Scott's olive skin tone, it's the only way he blushes. He dropped my other arm, too, like it was a stick of live dynamite. Both of my arms were free, and yet now I found myself leaning toward him too.

"Hi, Elizabeth," Gwen's voice called from behind me. "Glad we caught up to you."

Beauty barked a sharp, eager greeting.

I flung my sandals to the floor and slipped them on quickly. Then I turned to see Gwen leading the rest of my group to the table. "Oh, hi. Yeah, I got lost but found Scott here."

Other groups filed in around the other tables. Beauty wagged and licked at all who came near her, enjoying the fuss.

Alicia slid in beside Scott immediately, giving him a breathy "hello." Then she lowered her lashes and smiled, tucking her lips securely over her braces. She'd gone out with Scott before I did, and our friendship had floundered when Scott had dumped her for me. So it was an ego thing. She just had to try out her flirting powers on him again. And she was winning this time.

Scott grinned a big hello back. He seemed to enjoy all the attention he got too, just like my stupid dog.

"Hey Alicia, did you know Gwen and Scott are going out?"
I said casually. There—I'd warned her. If she kept up the eye-lash batting and the silly smirk, she at least would know she was making an enemy at her new school.

"Wow, what a small world." Alicia sat back, recovering quickly.

Gwen smiled at her, confident and secure, as she offered Beauty bits of a cookie.

I ended up talking to a lot of new kids, explaining about guide dogs and guide dogs in training. But when it was time to go, I stumbled over Beauty and ended up looking stupid yet again.

"I just can't walk in these shoes anymore," I complained.

"I'll lend you my gym shoes," Scott offered, and that was the end of the glamour part of my day. With his size 9 basket-ball hightops on, I kept tugging at my sundress as I sat in my classes, copying down all the things I needed and assignments due in my high-school planner. It was the secret to high-school success, after all. Mrs. Johnson had told us. Keeping it up to date was something I could handle. Not like high heels, Scott or Beauty.

Then, at the end of my first day at high school, I trudged home with Alicia and Beauty.

"Gwen's not in the least bit pretty," Alicia lied. "You just have to work a little harder. Find excuses to get together with Scott. Hey—she may have his heart now, but you've got his hightops."

"Uh-huh. Bye. See you tomorrow." Beauty and I continued on to our house. I sent her to her crate so I could sort through my homework alone, in my bedroom, in peace. There wasn't that much, first day and all, but I just wanted to stay organized. That's when I realized my day planner had gone missing. I felt hot and sweaty as I rifled through my backpack a third time.

"Elizabeth, is that you?" my sister's voice called.

"Who else?" I said dropping the bag.

"Could you come here? It's an emergency." Debra sounded as though she were stuck at the bottom of a tiny hole.

I went to see what was wrong.

"Liz!" She grabbed me the moment I stepped into the hall. "Thank god you're home. Come in here, quick, and shut the door." She pushed a little white tube into my hands. "Check out the windows," she told me. "What do you see?"

I studied the two clear slots in the tube and tried to be exact, since it seemed so important to Debra. "A blue heart in the left-hand window and a double blue line in the other."

"No!" Debra cried. "Do you really think that shape in the left window is a heart? I mean, do you think it's dark enough or is it just some shadow? It looks like a blob to me."

I studied it again. "It's definitely a heart."

"OK, OK. Tell me, a heart means *positive*..." She passed me a box, now, with a picture of a baby on it. "Could you double-check these instructions? Does that mean positively pregnant, or positively not pregnant?"

I looked from my sister's bruised face to the tube, and then to the tiny print on the box. I read the positive paragraph twice, to make sure I got it right. "You're having a baby," I finally said, feeling just as stunned as she looked.

Debra slumped back onto her bed, throwing her hands over her face. "What am I going to do?"

I sat down beside her and slumped back, covering my face too.

"I don't know, I don't know." Then suddenly I sat up. "First thing," I said, feeling a little sick now, "first thing, Debra, you're going to have to tell Mom. Does she know yet that you and Rolph have broken up?"

"Oh, my god."

I sighed, taking that as a definite no. "Could you just give me a few minutes to clear out first, then?" The last place I wanted to be was in the same house when Debra told Mom all her news. So, battered and bruised—on the outside from Rollerblading and on the inside from my first day at high school, and Debra's problems—I limped downstairs. "Walkies, Beauty? Do you want to go walkies?" I asked.

Beauty rushed at me from her crate, wagging her tail in a high-speed *thump-thump*. I dropped to the floor, giving her permission to throw her paws on my shoulders and slather my face. She was instant cheer-up medicine. Even though my eyes and mouth were tightly scrunched up for anti-drool protection and I couldn't see Beauty, I could still feel her massive, friendly paws weighing me down, making me feel secure and somehow more in balance with the world. I scratched behind her ears, stroked her back and then just threw my arms around her. She didn't care about anything or anyone else in the world in that moment but me. She didn't mind that Deb's problems would soon take over the house. It didn't matter that I'd tripped, that I'd lost my day planner and my sandal or that I still liked Scott. In Beauty's eyes, I was everything and I was perfect.

Beauty made a sudden break for the front door, grabbing one of Scott's hightops and shaking it.

"You're right," I told her. "We should get those back to him."

Find excuses to get together with Scott. It's what Alicia had advised me to do, and she had way more success with boys than I did. And Deb, my other expert, had told me Beauty attracted Scott. It seemed like a mutual thing, too.

So I headed over there, Beauty trotting alongside me, both of Scott's hightops in her mouth now. The last bit of sunset color was just draining from the sky and the air cooled quickly. I rang Scott's doorbell and hugged myself as I waited, trying to keep warm.

"Elizabeth, come on in," Scott said when he saw me. "You're shivering. What's wrong?"

"Oh, nothing. Just cold. Here, take these." I pulled the shoes from Beauty's mouth and handed them to him. "Actually, I lost my day planner."

"No!" Scott shook his head in mock horror, and then smirked. His voice turned into a falsetto imitation of Mrs. Johnson: "'The high-school student's most important tool to success.' How will you ever manage without one? Just one sec'y." Scott reached into the closet and pulled out his backpack. He rummaged for a minute and then held out his planner to me. "Here. I never use it." He chucked my shoulder and winked. "And I'm doing just as badly as in elementary school."

"Thanks so much… Hey, you wouldn't want to come for a walk, would you?" I asked.

"Sure." He grabbed his jacket. "Do you wanna borrow this?

I nodded and he draped it over my shoulders. I felt instantly warm and relaxed.

Outside with Scott, I looked up. The sky had purpled and one pinprick of silver winked at me. The first star of the evening. Would I ever feel this easy with another boy again in my whole life? I wished on that star. *Let me have Scott back.*

"Something else bothering you?" Scott asked after we'd walked without talking for a minute.

"Yeah. Although I really shouldn't say."

"Come on. Haven't we known each other our whole lives? I mean, there's no one for me like you. Don't you feel that way?"

"Yeah, I do, but you've got Gwen."

"Still, you and I are best friends." Scott put his arm around me. "And that means more." He drew me around to him and kissed my forehead. "Listen, Liz, let's make a pact. When we get really old—let's say when I turn thirty—we call each other up no matter where we are and, if we're not hooked up with anyone else, we get married."

I could feel all kinds of color rushing to my face. That had to mean that Scott loved me, right? "Didn't someone else do that in some movie?" I asked.

"Too bad. We're doing it too. And this will seal the deal."
Cupping my chin in his hands, Scott kissed me on the lips.

Kyle

Blind Man's Bluff

It sucked to rely on other people. I pushed open the bathroom door leading back out to the mall, hoping to find
Ryan outside waiting for me. But the first twenty people got
a free turn on Killer Commando—what was I thinking?

Could I shuffle my way back to the food court? I started forward, trying to sniff for food while brushing my fingertips along the wall.

"Hey, watch where you're going," a woman complained as I stumbled over some kind of carriage. When a
baby cried, I realized it must have been a stroller.

"Sorry."

I kept going, fingering sometimes open air, sometimes
clothing displays. Still no food smells. I could hear a water
fountain, and the *bing* of an opening elevator. Had to be
close by, if I remembered correctly. I doubled back toward
the smell of popcorn. My fingertips felt greasy from the
dirty walls, but I stumbled toward what I thought was the
Corny Combos stand. Somebody bashed into me.

"Ow. Oops—sorry!" Then I remembered that the popcorn concession wasn't part of the food court. Oh, where
the heck was I? I stopped and held my hand to my head.

"Hey, you're not going to throw up in here, are you?"

When I didn't answer right away, somebody grabbed my arm. He smelled vaguely of garlic and some kind of lime aftershave.

"Listen, I'm not drunk." I took a breath. I had to ask for help; there was no choice. "I'm blind. Would you just lead me back to the food court? There's a bunch of girls from my school there."

He started speaking a little louder. "Well, I just cleared out some female students. Loud and giggly. Would that be them?"

Mall security. Oh, great. "Probably."

"Sorry. My job, you know. They were taking up table space, and other people were waiting."

"OK, OK." I had to think quickly. "How about the arcade? Some guys I know are playing Killer Commando there."

"One-fifteen," he said, as though checking his watch. "My lunch break, but OK." He grabbed me by the elbow and we headed through the mall. Back when I could see, I used to feel sorry for the kids being dragged alongside security guards—caught shoplifters, I'd assumed. How many people might be thinking I was a shoplifter? What if one of them knew my parents? *It's more embarrassing to be blind than caught shoplifting*, I thought as we finally made it to the arcade. The security guard called out Ryan's name in a booming voice that made it sound like he wanted to arrest him.

Would he have even answered if he had been there?

Who knows? No one answered, in any case, and it wasn't like I could pull him out of a lineup. "Doesn't seem to be any Ryan here. What d'ya wanna do next, kid?"

I thought for a moment. "Call a cab. Do you know how much it would cost to get to Halton High?"

"Mmm, it's not so far. Ten bucks max." He spoke to someone else now. I guessed into a cell phone. "Ah, yeah, would you send a cab to the east entrance of Fairview Mall. Five minutes? Thank you." He spoke to me again. "I'll take you to the exit. Green cabs are fast. One should be waiting by the time we get there."

It's much quicker to walk when a security guard leads you. All the crowds part to let you through. Still, the guy was right about Green cabs being fast. The cab beat us. I could have made it back to school on time if only he'd been right about everything.

"Halton High—here you are," the driver announced when the cab rolled to a stop.

Ten bucks in my wallet. I fingered the bill. The tens I always fold in half. I handed the folded bill over in the direction of his voice.

"Hey kid, what do they teach you in school, anyway? Can't you read? The meter says fifteen."

"Oh, great." I shrugged my shoulders, suddenly exhausted with all the pretending. "You know what? I can't read, I'm blind. Could you just let me off with ten?"

"Hey, I gave at the office. If I let you off, I'd have to let everyone off. Equal rights, you know? Do you have a friend or a teacher who could lend you another seven? That would include a tip."

Could I do that? If I found someone really quickly, I could pay them back another day and my parents would never know. When you're blind, can you find anything really quickly, though? "My mom works at Terraview Motors." I sighed. "She'll give you the rest."

But of course, I had to drive with him there and we interrupted her with a client during the paperwork of a sale, something she hates. And there and back cost an extra ten dollars, as well as the rest of the next period at school. Apart from that, Mom would never have had to know about the cane folded up in the backpack—everything could have been fine. I could have almost handled the whole thing myself.

Almost.

For my last class, math, I needed a teaching assistant to help, since I couldn't see the board work and my Braille wasn't up to par yet. We sat at the back and she had to speak slowly so I could work out the answers to the equations in my head. It sounded like someone explaining something to the school idiot. I wanted to throw my textbook in the direction of her voice. So much for being myself and blending in.

After last period, a voice like silk spoke close to my ear.

"Where did you go at lunch?" The tangerine scent of Sunrise, coupled with the fact that no one else cared where I was at any given time, confirmed that that the voice belonged to Maddie. I hated the way everything inside me lifted and brightened at the sound of her voice. I wished I could control it.

"Where did I go?" I snapped.

"Yeah. Ryan said he saw you playing Space Invaders one moment, and the next moment you were gone."

"OK, Maddie. Just picture me playing Space Invaders. How exactly would this be possible?"

"Oh, my god, that Ryan's such a liar."

"Uh-huh. He left me in the washroom." I shook my head. "And I didn't even have my cane." I stopped, feeling my face turn red. Stupid. I didn't want Maddie to know I needed one.

"Well, you're OK. That's the main thing." I heard Maddie's sigh, like the soft rustle of leaves. Then she continued.

"Rebecca thought for sure you'd gone off and…" Maddie stopped talking. She shouldn't have stopped. She should have finished her sentence and then chuckled at the ridiculousness of Rebecca's suggestion.

"Gone off and what…killed myself? Geez, Maddie, in the middle of lunch hour? In Fairview Mall? I couldn't play Killer Commando with Ryan, so the world became too much for me?"

Maddie laughed nervously.

The thing is, back when the bandages had come off the second time, I had thought of killing myself. But no good way had ever come to me. Could I drive myself off a cliff? Tie a noose and position a chair? No, I'd probably need an

O & M instructor to help me. And then there had always been Maddie, her voice like silk, her touch like sunshine, making me feel like I was still worthwhile.

"Or did you think I killed myself over you?" I wanted to stay angry with her, to stop wanting her back. "What a laugh. You saw all the girls hanging onto me at lunch." Even to my own ears, I sounded pathetic.

She touched my cheek. I turned away. I remembered once fingering a bag of cookies, wondering if eating them all could put me in a fatal coma.

"You all think my life is so worthless just because I can't see."

"I'm sorry, Kyle," Maddie said, each word sounding heavy with regret.

"Don't be." I yanked her hand from my face but then I found I couldn't let go of it anymore. *God, no one will ever want to share this darkness with me*, I thought, and swallowed hard.

Of course, I couldn't see Maddie's face, but she finally pulled her hand away. "Do you need help getting to the parking lot?"

Not trusting my voice, I simply nodded.

When Mom had paid the cab driver at lunch, she hadn't said a word. She hadn't wanted to make a scene, after all, not with a SUV sale nearly in the bag. And in the car she never liked to argue. "I can't believe you," were the only words she said to me the whole way home.

Then, as she wrenched on the handbrake in our

driveway, she started right in. "What were you thinking, heading off to the mall without your cane?"

"I didn't do that on purpose. I forgot it. There was a whole gang of kids—I didn't need it, anyway." I stumbled out onto the driveway and headed toward the door. She didn't even help.

"You always need it! This episode just proves it!" she yelled from behind me.

"Not really. How much more would the cane have helped?"

I groped for the doorknob. "I don't know my way through the mall. I don't know my way home from the mall. I thought a cab was the best solution."

"What if I hadn't been in the showroom when you came? What then?"

"I would have gone from office to office with a tin cup," I told her. Mom was always in the showroom. She didn't even get out for lunch, she liked her sales so much.

"Oh, here, let me." She pushed my hand from the doorknob. I heard the door creak open. "We all have to get on with our lives now," she told me. "I need to know that you'll never wander away again. I just can't worry all the time."

I wanted to yell at her, *This is my problem, not yours!* Or maybe, *How exactly am I supposed to get on with my life now?* But there comes a point, whether you're blind or sighted, when you just want the lecturing to stop. So you stop arguing and say anything you think will end the nagging.

"Mom. Don't worry. I'll carry my cane everywhere from now on."

I hadn't even decided yet whether I was telling the truth or not.

Chapter 5

Elizabeth and Beauty

Good News, Bad News

Unfortunately, the major blowout did not happen while I was walking with Scott. Mom had decided to wait till Debra's pregnancy was confirmed by our family doctor before even bringing it up with Dad.

What with the five o'clock classes Mom taught, and Deb catching up with all her friends, it took till Friday for us to have our first family sit-down dinner. Friday was also the day the results became official. I could only guess which way it had gone by the special dinner Mom prepared. She served a rack of lamb, twice-baked potatoes and a squash casserole, all Debra's favorites.

Beauty paced back and forth, entranced by the wonderful smells. Debra, on the other hand, picked at her food as though searching for mold.

"Crate!" I commanded when Beauty placed one big paw on Debra's knee. She turned her huge brown head to me solemnly. *I'd rather beg than steal*, her golden eyes seemed to say.

Then she turned back to Debra, ignoring me.

"Beauty!" I snapped at her.

Slowly and mournfully she removed her paw and padded over to her crate.

"I don't blame the dog. This lamb is delicious, Debra, have you tried it?" My father asked as he scooped another helping from the plate in the center.

"No, no. I'm really sorry, I should have told you. While in L.A. I turned vegan."

"No eggs, no milk—at this time?" Mom screwed up her face in disbelief.

At what time? Was Mom going to tell us all about the baby now? Or had the pregnancy test been wrong after all? Maybe with this feast Mom was celebrating no baby instead.

She shook her head. "Debra, you really have to get your calcium and iron. You're too pale."

I looked at Deb. Was she really any paler than usual? I mean, she used to wear white foundation, so with that smoky-colored bruise around her eye, she looked more colorful than usual, if anything.

"Yes, of course, Mother," Debra said. Why did she sound so testy? "I eat a lot of soy products. They're really quite healthy. Very beneficial for a woman of your age, in fact."

Your age. Oooh.

"I have some good news," Dad suddenly broke in. Mom used to have a rule that we all had to share at least

one positive experience at the table. She'd wanted less
sniping, especially between Dad and Debra back during the
great university debate: "Yes, you're going." "No, I'm
not." Obviously Dad must have thought Mom and Deb
were closing in on a blow-up too.

"What is it?" I asked, hoping his experience wouldn't all
be in his usual computer babble.

"As you know, we had another re-org..." Dad paused as
he ate some potato. "Mmm, I love the sour cream and
cheddar cheese in here. You can't eat these then, eh, Deb?"
He reached over and stabbed into her potato, and dropped
it on his plate.

"No. But you shouldn't, either. They'll clog your arter-
ies—" Deb started.

"Is your position secure?" Mom broke in nervously.
Last year's re-organization of Dad's department had left
him without a job, at least for a while.

"Not only do I have a position, but I've been promoted.
Ten people now report to me." Dad smiled at my mother
and she smiled back.

"Congratulations. I'm glad they finally realized your
worth."

"Good going, Dad," I said.

"Ditto," Debra added.

"Let's break out the wine!" Dad said, leaping up. "I
think I have a really nice Chablis in the basement, saved for
just such an occasion."

"None for me," Debra offered. "It gives me headaches."

"I have to go out later, so maybe just a thimble," Mom said.

"Hey, can I have some? I survived half a week at high school."

"Yes, you may. Just get out the glasses," Dad said and headed downstairs to hunt down the Chablis. It took him a few minutes, but when he returned he cradled the bottle like a newborn.

"Where do we keep the corkscrew again?" he asked Mom as he placed his baby on the table. I set the glasses around it.

"Third drawer down."

Dad rattled and pawed. "Don't see it."

"Next drawer down, then. I have some good news, too." Mom talked over the cutlery rattling.

Here it comes, I thought, and took a deep breath as I listened.

"The CBC has announced its annual poetry competition. They want a suite of poems, or about twenty minutes of reading. Since the girls were little I've always wanted to enter but never got around to it. This time I already have six linked sonnets that my students all love. Another two should be enough."

I let my breath out. Phew, obviously there was no baby.

"Great, Mom. That'll be a snap for you," I said.

"Got it," Dad called, waving his corkscrew.

"I have a few months," Mom added. "Of course, it is marking time, and I want to shop with Debra for her wedding dress and trousseau. Who knows when we'll be able to get together again for that?...Which brings us to some other really exciting news. Debra, I think it's time to tell your father."

Wedding dress? Didn't she know about Rolph and Deb splitting? Uh-oh.

"Well, there's good news and bad news," Deb started. "I know we originally set the date for sometime in the spring and we had discussed June..."

"You're not putting the wedding off *again*," Dad said as he twisted the corkscrew around and around. The little metal wings on the side lifted up, higher and higher. "You've lived together almost two years. By now you really must be sure of each other."

"Yes," Debra said.

I sucked my breath in. Dad stopped twisting the corkscrew. Mom's mouth dropped open.

Debra shook her head. "The thing is, Dad, I am really sure about Rolph now, and I know I don't want to get married to him, ever."

Mom winced and threw up her hands as though giving up.

"Was that the good news or the bad news?" Dad asked.

"The good news is that I'm expecting a baby."

"Oh," Dad said softly. He jammed the metal wings down and the cork came out with a soft pop.

Woof! Beauty warned the cork from her crate.

"Fill 'er up," Mom said, pushing her glass toward Dad.

I was about to push my glass forward, too, but then the phone rang. I ran to grab the portable from the counter.

"Hello?" I walked with it to the family room.

In the background, Dad grumbled something not quite loud enough to hear. Deb answered, and Mom yelled out, "You can't raise a child by yourself!"

Beauty slunk to my feet for protection.

"Wanna come to the mall?" Alicia said on the other end.

"You don't even have a good education!" Mom continued.

Beauty whimpered. I plugged my non-phone ear. "You bet. Meet me at the bus stop in five minutes."

"OK." Alicia's voice sounded tiny.

Mom's still sounded big and angry. "I'm not raising any more children. She'll have to do it all on her own."

Beauty jumped up on me. "Don't worry, girl. I'll take you, too." I slipped on her green jacket and hooked her to the leash.

"I'm going to the mall with Alicia," I called back to the kitchen in a normal tone. In our house, a normal tone just fades into nothingness, especially when it's my voice.

Beauty and I made our break.

I felt pure relief when I saw Alicia at the stop. A friendly, non-yelling face! The bus pulled up almost immediately and we hopped on. Escape from the house of doom. But Beauty still seemed uneasy, pacing back and forth. "Settle, girl. Come on, lie down." Beauty sat for a minute, then stood until I pushed her down again. Her ears flew up with every ring of the signal bell and *sish* of the brakes, and she panted really hard the whole way.

"I think the arguing back home got to her," I explained to Alicia. Then as we walked into the mall I told her what the fighting was all about.

"Oh, my god. You're going to be an aunt!" Alicia squealed, leaping onto me and hugging.

Until she said that, I hadn't really thought seriously about Deb having this baby. "I...uh, me. I'm going to be..." I was Deb's little sister. How could I be old enough to be an aunt?

"What do babies really do, anyway? Cry?" In fact, at that moment we heard one screaming its head off in the babyGap store. How could anyone stand that sound?

Alicia let go of me. "What do you mean, what do they do? They're cute, Liz. They wear the most adorable things." She turned toward the store where the crying came from. Beauty lifted her ears and strained at the leash, ready to rush over to the rescue. Alicia smiled. "I know how to make the whole experience clear to you. We need to go shopping."

So Alicia led us over to the baby store, with Beauty wagging and grinning, just as eager as Alicia.

"Nice dog," the saleslady told us, a sure sign she wouldn't kick Beauty out. By law, guide dogs had to be allowed in all public places, but dogs in training did not.

"Thank you," I told her as we drifted farther in. We

passed the crying baby, who seemed to be falling asleep on a bottle in its stroller now. The sleeping baby looked pink and sweaty and very breakable.

"Isn't this the sweetest?" Alicia stopped at a display and picked up a yellow velour sleeper with a big white duck on the front.

"It's soft," I agreed, rubbing the material with my hand.

"And on special. Part of our back-to-school sale," the same saleslady offered. "Thirty percent off. Did you want help with the sizes?"

I shrugged my shoulders.

"That's a twelve-month-size sleeper. This one is a newborn." She held it up. Both Alicia and I stared for a moment.

"My baby's already into the twelve-month size," the crier's mom chimed in, sounding very proud. "He was nine pounds at birth, so newborn only fit him a short while."

Her son looked tiny! "We better take the twelve months." I just couldn't handle it if Deb's baby was even smaller than Screamer Boy.

"Shall I gift-wrap it for you?" the saleslady asked.

"No, no, that's OK." I decided I would keep it in my room, to help make the idea of Debra's baby more real to me.

"Over there. Look quick," Alicia told me when we stepped out of the store.

"Where? What?" I swung my head around. But then I saw him. I swear my heart swelled up in my chest and pounded like thunder. My husband-to-be in another fifteen years: Scott.

Then my heart shut down entirely and I couldn't breathe for a moment. My husband with another woman.

Beauty bolted forward. I dragged her back and ducked behind a pillar.

"What's wrong with you?" Alicia asked.

I told her about what Scott had said and how he had kissed me.

"So then why are you hiding?" Alicia asked. "Look, they're heading for the food court and I'm feeling really hungry about now."

"Well, I'm not!" I argued as she and Beauty dragged me along. Beauty was dying to follow all those fast-food smells.

The thing was I felt so stupid. I thought for sure, after that kiss, Scott would dump Gwen. I hadn't seen the two of them together at school over the past few days, either. But I had read the kiss wrong. Gentle and sweet as it was, it obviously meant nothing to Scott.

"Hi, Beauty!" Gwen called. There was no escaping the two of them now.

"Excuse me, Miss?" I felt a tapping on my shoulder. A security guard faced me. "Normally I'd let you eat in here. But some guy complained—said he couldn't eat around animals."

Kyle

Orientation and Mobility

"Y'all have a nice day?" Dad asked at suppertime after he told us how his big new case was going. Dad's a Scottish American in touch with his roots, and his Highland Piper Boys CD comes out when he feels stressed, just as his Georgian drawl does.

So with bagpipes playing in the background, Mom answered by recapping the day's disaster. Ever notice how everything sounds sadder to the tune of "Amazing Grace"? Still, she ended with what she thought was a positive spin. "Mr. Dietrich bought the extra option package for the SUV, even with the interruption. I'm definitely going to make the Automotive All-Star team this year, and Kyle's agreed not to leave the school grounds for lunch anymore."

"No!" I sputtered out a mouthful of mashed pota-toes. "I said I would always take my cane."

"But you also said you didn't know your way around, that your cane wouldn't have helped anyway."

I stabbed at my chicken leg, but bones are impossi-ble for me; the fork screeched across the plate instead. "Oh, Mom, come on." I snatched up the drumstick and shook it at her voice.

"Everyone heads for the mall at lunch. You want me to stay back at school like some freak?" I tore into the dark meat, caveman style.

"I watched Discovery Channel the other day,"
Shawna interrupted." And they had this show on dogs
that help handicapped people. Why don't we get one?"

"I'm not handicapped, I'm blind," I said, trying for
some more mashed potatoes.

"But you're chicken, too. That's a handicap."

"Am not. Quit kicking my chair." But she was right.
I was a chicken—afraid of the dark, afraid of being alone
and worst of all, afraid of dogs. You couldn't trust them.
One moment they were friendly, the next they would rip
into your face.

"Dad, they train the other kind of dogs, too—the
ones that guide the *vizzually challenged*." Shawna emphasized
the last two words to bug me. "Peas at two o'clock," she
said to me in a lower voice.

Peas are worse than chicken legs but both are in my
favorite-food category. So I stuck some mashed potatoes
on my spoon for glue and dipped it in at the two o'clock
position on my plate, hoping that none of the peas
would escape and roll all over the table like last time. I
think two actually made it to my mouth.

"Well, it seems to me you either get a dawg, or get to
know the mawl better," Dad said, his Southern drawl
dragging his words out. "Ah mean, so that you can find
your way around with a cane." With his big trial coming
up, Dad needed to settle this family thing quickly.

The Highland Piper Boys played "Flower of
Scotland" now. Over the whine of the music, I could

hear Dad's teeth clink into his fork—and both made my
fillings itch. "And since you can't get a dawg immediately, call your O & M instructor and get him to work with
you at the mawl."

Orientation and Mobility, his quick-pick solution.

"Until such time, your mama is absolutely right:
you must remain at school at lunchtime." *Click, click, click*.
Dad continued eating, totally satisfied with his decree.

The trouble was Jack, my O & M guy, was always
overbooked. It might take forever to snag him for a session. Did I want to be stuck alone at a table in the cafeteria every lunchtime till forever?

Mom rattled dishes and Shawna excused herself to
go to the bathroom. *The defense did not rest.* Instead I smol-
dered, trying to think of an opposing argument. I ate
slowly—didn't want to miss my mouth, after all. And
then I started again. "I never go to the mall by myself.
You know that. I mean, it's not like I can browse for
new fashions, right?" No one argued against me. Great.

"Really, it's just a matter of sticking with whomever
I'm with. I should have called out when I was in the
bathroom. Then Ryan would have remembered about
me and waited..." Still no rebuttal. Excellent, maybe I
could win this one.

"I'll carry more money on me, just in case. Really,
with the O & M instructors being so busy and all...well, I
just don't think we should waste Jack's time."

Dad's CD player was set on *Shuffle*. The Piper Boys

played "Amazing Grace" again, slowly and sadly. Still no one said a word, which was when it dawned on me: no one was left in the room. I'd been abandoned again.

"Sorry—what was that you said, Kyle? I just had to bring up the dishcloths from the laundry," Mom called from the other side of the room.

"Let me put in a new bag before you scrape your plate, Shawna," Dad said, I guess having just returned from dumping the full garbage into the can in the garage. *Shawna was the only one who excused herself from the table*, I thought angrily.

"Nothing, nothing." I sighed. I immediately called CNIB, even though it was closed, and left a desperate message for Jack.

*   *   *

Well, it turned out I was right. Jack really was over-booked. But at least he understood. As a special favor, he booked me a Friday-night appointment with Amber. Playing Blind Man's Bluff in the mall when a lot of kids from school might be there wasn't my first choice, but what could I do? When she introduced herself a couple of days later, at least Amber sounded young, although maybe a little too cheerful. If someone saw me with her, she might pass for a friend.

Even though she had driven in a car, she insisted we take the bus together. "That way when your girlfriend wants you to go shopping with her you can do it without your mom or dad driving."

She assumed I had a girlfriend, and for a bright, warm moment I saw Maddie sitting beside me on the bus. If I could only master this O & M stuff, maybe Maddie could see me as more than a blind freak who needed her help and pity.

For the first block, Amber gave me her elbow and spoke as we walked. "The bus stop is five blocks down, on the same side of the street as your house. We're coming to the first corner. Drop my arm and use your cane, now, please."

Tap, swish, tap. I hated it, wanted to fling the stupid stick in the sky. I'd have given anything just to keep holding onto someone forever in that darkness. Maddie, Maddie, Maddie.

Curb number two…three… At each one I had to stop and listen for cars. No traffic signals chirped a sure safe crossing for me at any of them. I half expected a car to plow into me whenever I stepped onto a street. Curb number four was the real biggie. It was a four-way stop with lots of traffic.

"Take your time here. Cars tend to watch for each other instead of pedestrians, at this kind of stop." Deep breath in. *Amber's right behind you,* I told myself. *She'll grab you if you walk in front of a car.*

Suddenly Amber yanked at my jacket sleeve. My heart whacked into my spine as I jumped back.

"Hey, relax. Where're you going? It's right here," she told me.

"But you didn't say it was on the fifth block, you said it was five blocks away," I snapped.

"We count differently—sorry," Amber said. "Bus is here, too," she chirped.

I heard the *sish* and *squeal.*

"To your left, three steps up."

One, two, three; I stepped up slowly.

"Good, good. You're doing great," Amber said.

Louder—come on, let's get everyone on the bus staring at me.

"Feel for the ticket box, that's it. Drop your coins in. Good!"

"How do I find a seat?" I whispered to her.

"Supper hour, Friday night—turns out they're all empty," Amber answered. "On your own, you'll just have to ask. Normally, lots of kids will get off at your school and the mall. But if not, just tell the driver and try to get a seat up front, so he'll remember to tell you."

Something I hated as much as my cane: relying on someone else to remember me. *O & M will give you independence.* Maddie, Maddie. Why did I feel so truly helpless? "I've been to this mall all my life," I complained to Amber when we entered the actual building. "I think I was born here."

"Great. Then we can zip through this stuff in a snap," she answered brightly. "What's your focal point?"

"Um, um, the water fountain," I answered quickly,

feeling my face heat up. It was where I used to meet
Maddie, back when I could see.

"Yup, good. But you know they do shut off the
water sometimes. You can't rely solely on the splashing
sound. It's just a clue. The structure itself has to be the
landmark."

"Shut off the fountain, yeah, right."

The sunshine girl ignored me. "This is a pretty easy
mall. One hundred and sixty-four stores. All pretty
much in a straight line, with the two major ones on
either end. Sears southeast and the Bay northwest."

There was no shortcutting Amber, easy mall or not.
First we counted walls and named them by direction and
number. Then she asked me to concentrate. "To your
left is an ATM. Can you hear it?" Amber asked.

"Uh-huh." I heard the arrogant beeps cueing cus-
tomers to key in more numbers, take their money and
remove their cards.

"Another sound clue," Amber explained.

"Yeah, they shut the ATM as often as the water
fountain," I grumbled as I kept going. *Tap, swish, tap.*

"You're veering to the right!"

Clunk. I bumped into someone tall. "Sorry!" I called.

"You just apologized to a pillar."

"Thanks for sharing, Amber," I said.

"My job. Hey, lighten up," she jabbed my shoulder.
"We all bump into things."

But you don't apologize to them, I thought. This has to work

for me. I chewed my lip as I walked away. Loud rap
music suddenly blared at me from my left.

> *You think you'll always love me*
> *But your love might fade away.*
> *Yo, yo, yo, yo. Think about it!*
> *I say, think about it.*

I veered away quickly. I didn't want to think about
my love fading anymore.

"That's Patches, a unisex boutique. Lots of kids
your age in there."

"I hate rap."

She ignored me. "Next a shoe store. Can you smell
the leather?"

I could. And then lots of sweet perfumey smells.

"A Body Shop," Amber continued. "How many
stores would that be?"

Oh, crap, could I remember? One hundred and
sixty-four stores in this place. "Bank, boutique, shoe
store, Body Shop. Four."

"Good memory! Water fountain, next."

I heard more voices. More people jostled me—or
was it me bumping into them? At least I apologized to
real people.

"Excuse me," *for taking up space in your sighted world.*
"Sorry," *for living.* "Pardon me," *for breathing your air. Get out of
my way, I can't see.*

The water rushed louder now—the sound clue, as
Amber had put it. *Bing!* I heard the elevator ring and

headed toward it.

"You're left-handed, aren't you?" Amber said.

"Why?" I snapped.

"Just a theory I have. You know, people who have trouble telling left from right—I find they're mostly left-handed. Can you feel for the button?"

"I don't have any trouble with left and rights," I snarled as I groped and then pressed a warm square. A slight draft and noise signaled the arrival and opening of the elevator door. I stepped in.

"Move right to the back," Amber told me. "There's a lady with a stroller coming."

Before I could move I felt a wheel roll into my ankle. *I know I'm blind, but what's your excuse?* I shuffled backwards.

Bing! We were off again. Chemicals, vinyl and leather, typing; two million women's clothing stores, all smelling and sounding the same.

Then I heard girls' voices, loud and clear. It couldn't be her—what were the odds?

"Amber, quick! Give me your hand and just play along!" I whispered desperately as I folded up my cane.

"Kyle, no. You don't understand."

"Please! Just move in closer. Pretend to be my girlfriend." I smelled a strange combination of cedar, coconut and wool as I put my arm around Amber.

"Aw, come back here, cutie," Maddie's voice called.

Who was she talking to? Suddenly, needle-sharp teeth sunk into my ankle.

"Ow, damn!" I shook my foot hard and a weight flung off my leg. *Yip! yip!* Dog cries. Cedar, coconut and wool—pet store, that's what those smells added up to.

"Aw, poor puppy," Maddie said. "Kyle, hi." I could hear surprise and confusion in her voice. "Aren't you going to introduce me to your...aunt, is it?"

CHAPTER 6

Elizabeth and Beauty

The Jackhammer

"Who complained about the dog? Where is the guy?" Alicia demanded as she scanned the crowded food court.

"Never mind, let's just go," I said, dragging her away. "I really didn't want to sit with them anyway."

"You don't get it, Liz. The more he sees the two of you together and compares, the sooner he comes back to you."

"Thanks, Alicia. But she's older than I am. She's sophisticated. And let's face it, she's hot." I jerked the leash to get Beauty to hurry out of the food smells. "C'mon, Beauty, let's go to the second floor and check out the pet store. You'll be welcome there, for sure."

On our way to the stairs, I noticed the crowd kind of parting around this tall guy in the distance. Something about him looked familiar. He wore sunglasses—even though it wasn't that bright in the mall—and dark clothes. "Oh, the guy from the park!" I said out loud.

"Kyle Nicholson? The blind dude with the attitude?

Haven't you seen him at school?" Alicia asked.

"No, I don't think so. I didn't know he was blind, either, till now." I watched him fling his cane from side to side as though he was angry.

"They say he went blind from diabetes just last year. Uh-oh, watch where you're going," Alicia said softly, just as the guy bumped into a pillar.

"Geez, he's bad with his cane. Why doesn't he get a dog?"

"I don't know. He's kind of cute, though. Why don't we just head over there and ask him?"

She would have done it, too, if I hadn't pulled her up the stairs instead. "You know, Alicia, maybe he doesn't like talking about it."

Still, I watched him continue on, with this older lady trailing alongside. My cheeks turned warm. I knew why I really didn't want to approach him. In a dark, don't-touch-me kind of way, he was cute. If I tried to talk to him, my face would turn even redder and my tongue would tangle around everything I said. Scott was the only guy I could talk to. Scott was the only guy for me. I just had to wait for him to break up with Gwen or for fifteen years to pass, whichever came first.

Beauty pulled me toward the pet store now, all excited. In the shop, cocker spaniel puppies wandered loose, yipping and wiggling, all happy to see Beauty. "Gosh, you're such a big dog compared to them." I said, stooping down. It made me sad to remember Beauty as almost that small.

Only another few months before she had to go. "Aren't they adorable?" I asked Alicia as one squatted and piddled beside me.

She nodded. "See, you like baby dogs—and what do they do? They whimper all the time and you have to clean up after them. Just like a human baby."

I frowned as I patted the piddler. A baby would link Debra to Rolph forever. A baby would take up her time and take her away from me. The puppy licked my hand. Puppies always loved me. I knew how and what to feed them. I picked out and paid for a rawhide bone. "Here, Beauty. You can carry your own treat."

I sighed. Sometime soon I would have to go home, where a certain baby was causing a lot of yelling. Alicia came from a normal family; she didn't understand. "What if I'm just no good with babies," I asked as we browsed the other stores, "like I'm no good with day planners, boys, makeup or any of the other things normal girls seem to know?"

Alicia shook her head and threw her arm around me.

"That's what you have your best friend for."

That made me feel better, and she helped me pick out a new tight orange T-knit. "Clashes with your hair and screams 'pay attention to me.' You'll see, Scott will come around."

I had my doubts, but bought the shirt anyway. Before we left, we needed to use the ladies' room, which wasn't too far from the food court. "Shh, Beauty, behave!" I tried to slink around the tables and chairs so the security guard wouldn't

turf us out a second time. We made it. Beauty insisted on
going into the stall with me and then she waited patiently at
my feet as I washed my hands.

As we headed out, the door flung open and the mystery
guy from the park stepped in. I stopped short and Alicia
bumped into my back. Beauty body-checked him, wagging
her tail hello and waiting for the pats everyone usually gave
her.

Kyle gasped, backed off and shoved Beauty away.

"My dog won't hurt you. She's only being friendly," I
told him. Dude with the Attitude. No wonder he was nick-
named that.

"Dogs aren't allowed in a mall," he grumbled. "What
the heck is it doing in here?"

"She's a future guide dog, which you could use," I told
him. "And at least she's in the ladies room. What the heck
are you doing here?"

"Mistake," he said, and fumbled behind himself for the
door handle. I could help him, but a crud like that—even a
good looking crud—deserved to struggle.

Alicia forced herself around me. "Here, let me," she
offered, and pulled open the door.

Turned out the older lady I'd seen him with was rushing
toward us to rescue him from his mistake. "Kyle, you headed right instead of left like I told you."

Kyle grumbled at her, too, but we didn't stay to hear it
all.

Alicia gave me a look as we headed to the bus stop.

"What?" I squawked at her. "Good girl, Beauty. Let me unwrap that for you and you can chew it on the bus."

Alicia shook her head. "If you were only as patient with humans as you are with people, you could have tons of boyfriends."

"What kind of guy doesn't like dogs?"

Beauty lay down innocently, her massive paws pinning down the bone as she sank her teeth into it.

"One that got boofed by a huge Lab when he didn't expect it," Alicia answered. "He can't see, remember? He had no idea what was hitting him."

"Uh-huh. Beauty, give that back for a sec. The bus is here."

We climbed up the steps of the bus much faster than we had on the way to the mall. Beauty walked to our seat and settled perfectly, head up expectantly for her treat. I gave it back to her and she chewed, noisily but happily, all the way home. At the bell signal for our stop, she woofed; but that was OK, she stopped immediately.

"Go, Beauty," I told her and she walked ahead normally, down the steps, through the door. A perfect, perfect dog. That Kyle guy was a stupid wuss.

Just as Beauty made the final jump from the last step to the sidewalk, a noise pierced my ears—sudden and awful, like an angry machine gun shooting holes in cement. I could almost see the ground shake, too. A man had started up his jackhammer.

Beauty leapt up and struggled, yelping as though one of

the machine-gun bullets had hit her. Then she broke away,
dragging her leash behind her.

"Alicia! Oh, my god, I have to catch her."

I flew after Beauty, not waiting for Alicia to answer.
Where the heck did Beauty think she was going? I caught up
to her in a flash, just as the bus pulled away, making even
louder *sishes*. I threw myself at the handle of her leash.
Missed. Beauty, wild-eyed and confused, dashed into the
street, right in front of the bus.

Kyle

The Drive

"Hey, man. Saw you at the mall with the older woman.
Come sit down at my table and tell me all about it,"
Ryan said at Monday lunch break.

"Aw, geez. It was a mistake. Honest, Ryan, how old
was she?"

"'Bout as old as my mom."

"Just shoot me, please," I groaned.

"Kidding, kidding. She wasn't too old for me.
Mind you, I like my women experienced." Ryan nudged
me. "And I like my women young." He whistled low.
"Over near the trays in the cafeteria line. Check out that
niner."

"Think about it, Ryan. It's not as if I can really do
that." I sighed. "Let's face it, you like your women any

way you can get them."

"Got that right. But you know, that older chick, she wasn't bad. Who was she?"

I broke down and explained how Amber was my O & M instructor. I told him how my last-ditch effort to make Maddie jealous had backfired. And how, to top it all off, when I thought I had the whole mall memorized and insisted I could go to the can by myself, I ended up in the girls' room.

"Ah, you know, you got this whole independence thing wrong. Chicks like looking after guys. Fact is you're a chick magnet. What are you doing this weekend?"

"I don't know—catching up on math if my mother has time to help me."

"Ouch, no, man! Come to my party. In fact, I gotta make a beer run. Let's go now. You can be a big help."

I heard his chair scrape back and wondered if I should head off with him. Who knew where he might leave me this time? I stood up.

"Hey, Maddie," I heard him call. "Wanna come to my party this weekend? Kyle really needs you to get him there."

I wanted to plow Ryan one, but then I smelled tangerine Sunrise and fought myself not to light up like a computer screen. He couldn't be right, could he? She wouldn't want to come just to help me around.

Maddie spoke to me directly. "You're not going to Ryan's party. It'll just be a drunken orgy. What fun could you possibly have?"

I grinned. "You make it sound so good."

"Don't be an idiot. With your diabetes, you can't drink anyway."

"Oh, no? Put a bottle in my hand and watch me."

"No, thank you!"

"I'm not dead yet, Maddie. I know you think my life is worthless. But you're wrong. I'm going to have the time of my life at Ryan's."

I waited for a bit. Had she left? I couldn't smell tangerine.

"Never mind her," Ryan told me as he grabbed my elbow. "We have a date with the beer store." He jingled his keys all the way to the parking lot. "Get in, get in, it's unlocked."

I fumbled for the door handle and pulled. Then I slid in.

Ryan started the engine and we drove away. "My dad's car. Two thousand two Mustang convertible. Says he'll give it to me as a graduation present."

"You're so lucky. I'd give anything to be able to drive, never mind get a Mustang just for passing."

"Anything? Damn, think I forgot my wallet. Here, take the steering wheel a sec while I check."

"What? Are you crazy?" I groped for the wheel and held it steady for a moment.

"Nope. Got it. Thanks." Ryan took the wheel again. "You'd give anything to drive, eh? Well, then, do I have a deal for you. I'll get carded if I try to buy a two-four. You with your Stevie Wonder act—I figure you can con someone into buying it for you."

"No way."

"No? Here I thought I'd take you to the church parking lot, put the top down, hand you the keys... "

"Me drive your Mustang? I swear you're certifiable!" I paused. It occurred to me that the beauty of Ryan was that he just had no clue about anything, let alone what I could or couldn't do. "Fine, I'll try to get you your beer. But only for ten minutes. If no one comes or agrees, you've gotta let me drive anyway."

"OK, bro." He turned into a parking lot and stopped the car. "I'll take you to the door and then you just wait for your mark.... "

"But I can't see when someone approaches me!"

"Right, right. I'll stand over to the side and whistle, like this." Ryan made a warbling sound. Like a cardinal.

"It's not going to work," I grumbled.

Ryan just jingled his keys.

I shook my head. How stupid did I feel standing there, white cane in hand? The white cane, of course, being Ryan's idea. I might as well have held out a tin cup and begged for the beer money, too. And I'd worried about walking the mall on a Friday night with my O & M lady. What if the wrong person came by today—say a teacher, or the principal? It seemed like hours went by before Ryan finally whistled.

"Excuse me," I started. Was it a man or a lady in front of me? "I need a case of twenty-four beers. I have the money, it's just I can't see and it's so hard for me to—"

"What brand?" a lady's voice asked.

I thought quickly about what kind Dad always drank and just asked her for that. "Here's the money, ma'am. Thank you so much." After she took the bill from my hand, I half hoped she'd just take off with it. That would teach Ryan about milking a handicap like that. But no, after a while she handed me the change and helped me tuck my fingers around the handles of the box.

"You sure you don't need help getting that somewhere?" she asked.

"That's OK. I'm expecting a ride any minute. Thanks again." I felt guilty and angry. Why did the lady have to sound so sorry for me?

"Here, let me take that for you," Ryan said to me.

"Don't even say a word. That was humiliating," I told him as he dragged me back to the Mustang.

"Oh, man, if you only knew. That chick was such a babe!" Ryan told me.

"Really?"

"Uh-huh. And now you are in for the ride of a lifetime."

After a short drive the car stopped and we switched places.

"Just unlatch that hook on the top of your windshield, Kyle."

What stupid hook? I thought as I felt around. I finally found a handle. "This one?"

"Yeah, just give it a yank."

I pulled at the handle.

"Great!"

I heard a soft buzz and then felt cold air rushing all around me. I couldn't help smiling. I heard a fizzy bubbling. "Aw, Ryan, you're not having one now...."

"Hey, I'm drinking, you're driving. The gas is on the right, brake's on the left."

I put my foot on the left pedal.

"The engine's still running. Let me just get the hand brake. OK. Put your hand on the gear, slide it back one notch, perfect. Release the brake, and you're motoring."

More cold air rushed past my face, whistled past my ears. I must have been driving less than ten miles an hour, but with the windchill factor, it felt faster. Not quite like surfing in Waikiki, but still wonderful.

"Turn right...and right again. Whoa, whoa, easy, stop. There's a squirrel in front of you."

I pounded my foot down on the brake and felt myself thrown forward.

"Great, great." Ryan chuckled. "You're better than my sister. Next time you'll parallel park."

CHAPTER 7

Elizabeth and Beauty

Depressed

The bus stopped within a whisker's length of Beauty, so she came out of her close call without a scratch.

At least on the outside. On the inside, Beauty was a wreck. I slammed the door behind us when we got home and she jumped like she was dodging a bomb. Mom clattered pots as she emptied the dishwasher and Beauty ducked into her crate.

I wanted to tell Mom what had happened to Beauty, but she was muttering as she dumped cutlery into the drawer. "Diapers, formula, no sleep at night, I'm not going through that again." She slammed the drawer and Beauty yelped.

"What is wrong with that dog?" she yelled.

I wasn't going to talk to her while she was in that mood. "C'mon, girl." I snapped my fingers at Beauty and she winced, shrinking into a corner of her crate. "Sorry, I didn't mean to scare you. You don't want to spend the whole evening there all by yourself, do you?" Finally she slunk out of the crate and followed me up the stairs.

I stopped outside Debra's door when I heard crying. Beauty's ears lifted and she turned her head toward me as though asking what we should do. I shrugged my shoulders and pushed the door open.

"Deb, I bought you something." I held out the babyGap bag and Deb looked up from her pillow. She wiped her eyes and sniffed as she took the bag.

"What is it?" She peered in. Slowly, slowly I saw her lips and cheeks lift. It was like watching the sun rise on someone's face. She took out the sleeper and tears streamed down from her eyes again. "Oh, my gosh, Liz. It's beautiful. You're the only one who understands. I love you." Deb grabbed me by the shoulders and hugged me.

Understand—who me? I felt guilty for a moment. Alicia had suggested shopping for baby clothes. *She* was the real girl, the one who understood boys and makeup and babies and, in this case, my sister. But I felt Debra's shoulders shake above mine and I tried to imagine a feeling for her baby, mentally picturing a puppy in a yellow sleeper. *No matter what,* I thought, *at least I can always try to understand.*

"Mom says I don't know what it's like to raise a child. That there are plenty of couples out there who could do a much better job of raising and loving my baby."

"No! She wants you to give it up?" It was exactly what Mom always made me do with my dogs. How could she expect that of Debra? I started crying now too.

I'd wanted to keep the outfit in my room until the baby
was born, but I could see that Debra needed it more.
Eventually, Deb actually fell asleep clutching it so I sent
Beauty to her crate and went to bed myself.

Next morning, when I got up and headed for the
kitchen, I found Mom already sitting at the table, writing
longhand on a yellow pad of paper. As I stepped in, she
ripped off the sheet she'd been working on and crumpled it
into a large, flower-like ball. She pitched it behind her and
it tumbled to join a garden of other yellow flower balls.

"Already it's started. I can't work." She looked up at me.
"I'm trying to write the last two sonnets for the CBC con-
test. But they should be on the same theme as the other six.
And I can't get back to that headspace."

She sounded so much like Debra when she talked like
that. I picked up one of the flowers, uncrumpled it, and
read something about dying leaves, sorrow, darkness and
death. Kind of grim. Probably a good thing that she could-
n't get into that kind of headspace, if you asked me.

If Beauty could write poetry, though, I thought, *she could continue
in Mom's theme.* She was still so depressed. I looked toward her
crate. "Beauty? Don't you even want to go outside, girl?"
She got up slowly and came to me, looking at me accusing-
ly. I gave her a treat, but she sniffed first and ate it slowly.
"Come on. There are no jackhammers in the backyard."
We went out through the patio door.

The sun shone bright white outside. It was a fall morning that glowed, it was so perfect. I threw the stick for

Beauty a few times and finally, by the third time, she actually wagged her tail as she returned with it. Good, she'd snapped out of it.

"Business, Beauty," I told her—the command for her to go to the bathroom. After she squatted I took her back into the house, confident she would be OK again. But instead of following me, she headed straight to her crate. Still not over last night.

That's when I noticed Deb sitting in the family room, reading the Saturday newspaper. What was she reading? I joined her in the family room to grab the comics and saw her circling apartment ads in the classifieds. Great, I thought. Just when I thought I had my big sister back; no Rolph. What was the point of imagining and bonding with the crying creature in a yellow sleeper? I was going to lose it all.

Breakfast started the fighting all over again, too. Mom insisted that Deb eat dairy and eggs. "If you want to have this baby, you can start making sacrifices."

Dad backed Mom up. "You can't experiment with nutrition now, Debra. Your baby's health is at stake."

"Fine." Debra shoveled some scrambled eggs into her mouth. "Can I borrow the car today? I need to check out some apartments."

"What?" Dad looked at Mom and then back to Deb. "You can't leave. At least not for the first year. Tell her." He looked at Mom again. "It's too hard."

"But there's no room here!" Deb said. Her voice was

just loud enough to start Beauty cowering in her cage. She whined softly.

"We'll build out the basement."

Mom gave Dad a sour look.

"We'll take out a renovations loan." He spoke to Mom now. "You've always wanted your own space. You can turn Deb's old room into an office."

"I've always wanted time for myself. And now, finally, for the first time in my life when I have it, this happens." Mom flung up her hands.

Debra tapped her chest with her index finger. "But it's *my* baby, *my* responsibility. You won't have to look after it."

"Oh, really? I'm already going to your doctor appointments. You have an ultrasound on Monday. I'll have to get someone to cover my classes."

"Don't!" Debra said. "I don't want you there." Then she stomped up the stairs back to her bedroom. Beauty began whimpering.

"What is wrong with that dog?" Mom asked.

I shrugged my shoulders. "Shh, shh, girl, it's all right. Come and eat." I grabbed the Dog Chow bag from the cupboard, shook it and poured some into her bowl—the regular drill. Still she wouldn't come. So I held out a bit of Deb's eggs to coax her out of the crate.

"She's been moping like that all morning," Mom told me as she watched.

"Yeah, well. Maybe all the fighting is getting to her," I said.

"All families argue. Blind ones too. She should be used to it by now. Maybe you should call Canine Vision."

"No!"

Mom raised an eyebrow at me.

I sighed. "OK, OK. Beauty got spooked by a jackhammer when we got off the bus last night. But she'll get over it. She just needs a little time."

Beauty picked over her food, looking for bits of egg. When she couldn't find any more, she gave Mom a white-eyed look and then backed into her crate again.

Her tail flip-flopped just a little inside her cage when the door bell rang, and she raised herself up halfway.

I answered the door. "Gwen?" I said, stunned.

"I'm sorry, I should have called, but Scott said you wouldn't mind. I brought *Camel on a Skateboard* for your sister to autograph."

Hmm, she might be the right person to cheer Debra up. "Step inside. I'll go upstairs and get her."

Beauty didn't follow behind me, and that was so weird, like losing my shadow. I knocked on Debra's door and then called "Deb? A fan here to see you."

"What?" I could hear pleasure in her voice. It was as though I had told Mom some student had called to say he'd loved her poems. The door opened.

"Scott's girlfriend is waiting in the family room. She wants you to autograph her copy of your book."

"All right." Deb winked at me. "I'll check her out for you."

I grinned. Deb always knew how to be a good big sister. And I wanted to do something back. "Listen, Deb, if you want company, I'll go with you to that ultrasound Monday."

"That would be nice," she said squeezing my shoulder. Then we went down to the family room together. Debra signed Gwen's book and chatted with her about the techniques and materials she used on it.

I lay down near Beauty's crate with my head beside hers.

"What's wrong with her?" Gwen suddenly called, when she noticed where I was.

"Nothing, nothing, she just had a scare last night." I told her about the jackhammer shaking up the walk just as Beauty stepped on it.

"Really?" Gwen nodded. "Poor thing. I once had a dog who heard a firecracker go off and refused to go out at night ever again."

"Why don't you call the trainer?" Debra suggested.

"Because they might ask for her back right away."

"Ohhh," Gwen said. "You should give Scott a call. I bet he could think of a way to cheer Beauty up. He's crazy about her. Talks about you two all the time."

"My goodness," Debra said slyly. "You're awfully trusting with your boyfriend."

"Yes, well, I know he thinks of Liz as his little sister."

I felt my face flame up and couldn't trust myself to say anything back. When the phone warbled twice to signal long distance, I was happy to run and answer it.

"Hawow, Deb?" A slurred voice called.

My heart froze. It couldn't be. "This is Elizabeth," I answered.

"Little sister," the voice sputtered. It didn't sound like Rolph at all. For an artist, he had always seemed too much in control, and he usually spoke in crisp business-speak. "Could you just halp me out? Get your sister to talk to me. Tell her I lawwve her so bad. I just need her to give me a chance, yah know?"

Kyle

The Party

"Aren't you ashamed of yourself?" Maddie cornered me after class that afternoon. "Ryan's bragging all over school how you got someone to buy beer for him."

"What do you care?" I asked, grinning inwardly, because it was great knowing she did.

"You think I want you to turn into some kind of loser just because I left you? What do you think I am?"

"Like you make or break me? I'm not turning into a loser, Maddie. I just drove a Mustang at lunchtime. And this weekend, I'm going to have more fun than I ever had with you." I tried to walk away from her then, but I didn't want to hit her with my cane. So I turned around and bumped into the wall.

"Did you hurt yourself? Here, let me help." A girl's voice spoke at me and a soft hand touched my shoulder.

"It's Rebecca." She pulled me away from the wall.

"Rebecca?" I repeated. Maybe Ryan had the right attitude about my blindness. Maybe I should just milk it. I smiled at Rebecca, as though bumping into walls agreed with me. "Do you mind escorting me to my math class?" Rebecca didn't mind at all. And when I asked her to come to Ryan's party later in the week, she even said she would drive. So there, Madison, I can too live without you.

I asked my little sister to give me the once-over to make sure my shoes matched and I didn't have any toothpaste on my shirt. When Rebecca came to the door, I heard Shawna's low whistle of approval.

"Kids." I shrugged at Rebecca as I took her arm. "You want me to drive?" I asked.

Rebecca laughed too hard and long at that one. "That's a good one. Ha, ha! What a great sense of humor!" The car shrieked as we pulled out of the driveway. I liked that. It's what I would have done. As we drew closer to Ryan's house, we could already hear the music blaring.

> *Poom, poom-chhh. Poom, poom-chhh.*
> *You think you really love her,*
> *but your love may fade away.*
> *Poom, poom-chhh.*

Only one song in the whole universe. The radio played it constantly and every time I heard it, I swear the rapper sounded angrier and angrier. I liked that about

him and found myself starting to like the song. It was
such a long rap, too, that even after we'd parked and got
Rebecca's stash of beer into a cooler, we still had time to
dance to it. "Think about it, think about it!" I yelled out
when the rapper sang the chorus.

For supper I had eaten only vegetable soup and taco
salad, hold the taco—this to save some carbos for the
party junk I might snack on. Mom insisted. When Ryan
forced a beer into my hand, I realized I might have to
use up my carbo allowance on this bottle.

Chug-a-lugging as I swayed from foot to foot, I
almost gagged. *Bleah*, why did anyone drink this stuff? It
bubbled bitter all around the sides of my mouth. I even
felt the bubbles in my jaw joints up into my ears. But
I did feel thirsty, and if I just drank the one, Ryan
wouldn't make a big deal.

Somehow, when I put the empty down, another
full one ended up in my hands. We danced slower and
slower, Rebecca's body pressed warm into mine, and
this bottle didn't taste nearly as foul as the first.

"There's a guitar on the shelf there." Rebecca
paused as though she was pointing.

"Yeah, OK, so there's a guitar over there. Do I look
like Jeff Healey?"

"Who's that? No, I just heard you play at the
assembly last year and I thought you could maybe sing
something for me."

I shrugged my shoulders to mean, *Oh sure, someday,*

when I get around to it. But Rebecca dragged me to a couch
and replaced my beer with the guitar.

By that time I felt really good—maybe even a little
buzzy. I strummed and tuned the thing for a bit first.
Then I really put everything into a song I had written for
Maddie. It made me a little sad, but when I finished it
wasn't only Rebecca clapping.

"Hey, man, sing another one, you're making the
chicks mellow." Ryan's beery breath blew out at me. So
after a beer break I sang another. The girls kept asking
for more. Finally I started rapping that stupid song all
the radios were constantly playing, but I made up my
own words.

> *I thought you'd always love me*
> *But you dumped me in a day.*
> *Think about it. Think about it.*

Everybody joined it on the last line and they sounded just as angry as I did.

> *You kissed me like you meant it*
> *But your heart had gone astray.*
> *Think about it. Think about it.*

I had another big gulp of beer.

> *I thought my life was over*
> *When I watched you walk away.*
> *Think about it. Think about it.*

The chorus boomed so loud around me, I swear I
could feel the vibrations up through my feet.

> *Then I found another woman*
> *And I found I still could play.*

This time, as the chorus welled up around me, I yelled out, "And now I'll never have to think about it again!"

Woo-hoo! Everyone laughed and cheered. "Hey, you're really great, man!" "I like your version of the song better." "You should send in a demo to the radio."

Ah, what did they know? Still it felt good, even if my head was cottony and my stomach swirled. After another beer and another couple songs, Rebecca told me her curfew had been about ten minutes ago. "Jus' a second darlin', I need to go tinkles." I tried to get up by myself but my roadie grabbed my arm right away and led me to the bathroom.

"Thanks, Becky, you're a real peach." Those were my last words before I hurled.

I didn't feel nearly so bad when I'd finished and I thought, *Hmm . . . maybe I won't even need an extra shot of insulin, now that all those carbos are in the bowl-o.* I washed up and rinsed out my mouth with water.

"Do you have a stick of gum?" I asked Rebecca when she drove me up to my house.

"No, but here's a mint." She pushed a round, smooth candy into my mouth before I could tell her how much I hated mints.

"Uh, thanks. Thanks for everything," I said and

kissed her lightly at the door. Then I grabbed hold of the handle, pressed down on the latch and pushed through.

"Hey, hey! Come out, wherever you are. I'm home and wasted," I called as I stumbled into the entranceway. No one answered. What? No one had waited up?

Well, that was certainly fine with me. Just perfect, matter a fact. I was gonna get away with getting smashed, for cryin' out loud. This was great. As I tripped over some shoes, the bathroom door creaked open. *Whoops, who is it?* I wondered.

"You smell," Shawna complained at me. My luck was holding out.

"I know you are but what am I?" I answered back. *Why doesn't that make any sense?* I wondered, the moment the words left my lips.

"You're drunk."

I took a deep breath, belched and then gave her the best zinger comeback my cottony brain cells could think of. "So what?"

"Sooooo…I'm telling."

I ignored her, headed for my room and, as dozy as I felt, pricked my finger for my nightly blood-sugar test. Damn, that hurt—always did, no matter what. I tried to squeeze my blood onto the test paper, but bled almost everywhere else. Then I dozed for a minute, waiting to hear what the voice box attached to the Glucometer would say.

NOT ENOUGH BLOOD, it finally announced.

Damn, I had to prick my finger again. This time I squeezed the blood right into the divot on the strip. *Take that, you vampire.* I felt pretty rotten by now—exhausted, like I could sleep forever, and headachy. The mallets had returned, pounding on the back of my useless eyes. A minute passed, and the vampire spoke again, loud and clear.

CALL THE DOCTOR.

"Yeah, right. Like he's gonna answerrr at two in the morning." I stumbled back to the door. "I'll just walk all the carbos off. That's what I'll do." I grabbed my cane and *tap-swished* back down the hall, out the door and down the walk. Block one, block two—I had no problem crossing the intersections tonight. No sirree. Block three, block four. Oh man, what was happening to me? Suddenly, a million knives jabbed into my brain cells. *I juss have ta sit down, right here.*

I folded my legs and then felt myself sliding, melting...and then nothing.

CHAPTER 8

Elizabeth and Beauty

Dog Therapy

"I'm sorry, I can't help you," I told Rolph. Well, Deb was chatting away with Gwen, having a good time. Was I going to interrupt that, so she could talk to a drunk? How embarrassing would that be for her, with Gwen sitting right there, even if he had something to say that she wanted to hear?

I hung up.

"Wrong number," I lied to no one in particular and smiled.

"Maybe I will give Scott a call," I told Gwen. *Let's just see if he thinks of me as a kid sister.* "He can help me walk Beauty. If we carry her part of the way, and there's no noise, she should get over it eventually."

"Great. If you want to take her over to Scott's now, I'll come with you," Gwen said.

Turned out Beauty was far too heavy to carry, but we coaxed as we dragged her. "Look how nice it is outside, girl.

Not too hot, not too cold." She looked up at me and stepped forward slowly, tail hanging. When we finally got to Scott's, it took ten dog biscuits to lure Beauty on to Gwen's house.

Which is when Scott kissed Gwen good-bye, as I watched. Slow, easy, his lips gentle on hers—that kiss looked no different from the one we'd shared. What exactly did that mean? Were we getting married in fifteen years or not? I had the feeling Scott didn't know either, and we had nothing much to say on the way home after that.

It took only two biscuits to walk Beauty back. *At least she's getting over the jackhammer*, I thought as we turned down our walk. But then a bus rumbled up behind, *sishing* just a little as it slowed down for the stop sign. Beauty bucked like a wild bronco. When I got the door open, she bolted for her crate.

By Saturday, I was still bribing her and dragging her on short walks. Always there would be a bus, and Beauty would drag me straight home. Mom happened to be at the house for Beauty's daily dash to the crate. "If she doesn't like walks anymore, how can she possibly be a guide dog? You have to call Canine Vision, Liz. Don't put it off any longer."

I squeezed my eyes shut and swallowed hard. It was so unfair. Beauty had been the perfect dog until that jackhammer. Now she didn't even make a good pet. She hardly wagged her tail anymore; she didn't jump up to greet me.

I sat beside her crate and stared into her sad golden eyes.

"I'll try to keep you if you flunk, girl. You know that I'll always love you." She licked my face with her warm tongue and made me feel better.

So I made the call. I didn't get through to the head trainer right away, but I did leave a detailed message about Beauty's problem. He called me back later and I explained how Beauty acted around buses—and any loud noises, really, since that jackhammer.

"What a tough break. We should really take her back right away. Maybe we can retrain her."

"No! Please, whatever you do I could try here at home."

"Well, it's a long shot, and it means a lot of work for you."

I couldn't give Beauty up like this. I didn't want to give her up at all, when it came right down to it. But to abandon her when she was depressed and disgraced? Never. "I want to try. Anything."

"All right. What you have to do is gradually accustom her to noise in positive situations. So when you feed or play with her, do it with lots of sounds around her. Start with a drum—beat it softly as she eats. Talk to her, calm her. Then beat the drum louder. Later, you can tape the sounds of the bus and play them. Build up to jackhammer sounds. Do you think you can handle this?"

"Yes," I said, crossing my fingers. I remembered Beauty's white-eyed panic when that jackhammer began, her trembling and her million-mile-an-hour heartbeat. And I knew how she acted now. She wasn't even the same dog. But I couldn't say no to the trainer, because it would be like losing faith in a best friend.

"Elizabeth, some dogs recover from this kind of fright. But no matter how hard you work, Beauty may not. Just do your best."

I swallowed hard as I hung up, and decided that no matter what, I would never give up.

Next I called Scott, and he came over immediately with his bongo drums.

He put on the radio so he could beat the drum to some music. The plan was I'd offer Beauty biscuits close to the drum. Scott patted the skin softly. Hardly more than a plop sound came out.

"It's OK, Beauty. Good girl. No one's going to hurt you." I threw a bacon-flavored mini bone outside her crate so she would at least step out, but she just ignored it. "There are dogs going to bed hungry all over this world, you know." That was desperation talking—actually, more like Mom. And it was useless, anyway, to reason with a depressed Lab.

But then we had a tiny breakthrough. Beauty's favorite Elvis tune started on the radio. Her ears lifted up and she stepped out of the crate.

"All right, Beauty!" Scott dropped to his hands and knees, wagging his own butt. Beauty's lip lifted and she started to wag too. Scott motioned for me to grab the drums. I played along softly, but she didn't even notice. I hadn't seen Beauty so happy in a week. When Scott started to howl so did Beauty, but it was with pure joy. By that time I was pounding the bongos and she still didn't care.

When the song ended, I gave Beauty the same treat she had ignored before, and she crunched it all down with her usual grin. "Good girl, Beauty," I said.

"So now all we have to do is slip a headset on her and walk her to Elvis's songs everywhere we go." Scott smiled.

He was teasing, but I snapped my fingers. "You're right! I mean, we can bring a tape player."

"Sure!" Now Scott sounded excited too. "And eventually we can add some sound effects."

"If she hears 'You Ain't Nothing But a Hound Dog' playing on the bus with a jackhammer..."

"She'll be cured!" Scott finished my sentence.

I felt so happy I threw my arms around Scott and kissed him. He ended up kissing me back. Mmmm...I forgot everything for a while, until Beauty nuzzled at my hand.

Scott pulled away first and cleared his throat. "Why don't we try out our theory right now?"

"Um, all right, sure," I said and tracked down my player to Dad's workbench. The batteries were old and we still had to tape the song from Dad's CD. It turned out to be a pretty poor reproduction. Still we set off, *not* dragging Beauty for the first time in a week.

She wagged her tail as she trotted along, glowing like the September sun, all bright and happy again. We walked block after block like that, all the way to the park. The battery did die, but by that time Beauty didn't seem to care as she sniffed trees and bushes, newfound old friends.

Then we heard the squeal of tires in the distance.

Beauty started shrinking into herself, as though she was gathering force to spring off in the other direction. "Easy girl, easy," I said to her. A souped-up Mustang convertible with oversized tires peeled out around the corner. As the car rumbled closer, I could hear the stereo pumping out a rap song. *Poom, poom-chhh. Poom, poom-chhh*. High on bass, low on melody. *You think you'll always love her, but your love may fade away*. The singer's voice sounded angry. But remarkably, Beauty held her ground. After a moment, she even wagged her tail. I realized then it didn't have to be Elvis singing to make Beauty happy. "Oh my gosh, Beauty. Don't tell me you actually like rap!" But it was clear she really did.

On the way home, Beauty walked at her usual brisk pace. Still, had I thought of it I would have stopped at the variety store for some more batteries.

"I guess you need to take her on a bus ride now. Well, I'll see you at school," Scott said. He looked at me and I knew he wanted to kiss me. I saw the white spots in his cheeks show up. So I reached up and kissed him. Gwen could go suck an egg.

Sunday morning I woke up really early and couldn't sleep. That's when it hit me. Batteries. Just to keep Beauty on the right track, I should go to the convenience store with her and get some. There wouldn't be any buses or construction noises now. Then I could bring her on the bus to the ultrasound Monday. I slipped on my jeans and a sweater and rushed downstairs to visit her.

"Hey, Beauty!" I whispered, half scared she'd only give me her depressed stare. But she leapt up, wagging. "Good girl. Wanna go for a walk?"

Beauty rushed me, tossing me over. Great.

I got up and rattled her leash and she wagged harder. She even barked. "Shh! It's still dark out. They'll think we're crazy!" I grabbed the tape player from the bookshelf.

Without the sun the air felt sharp, with a cold bite to it. "Hey, Beauty, I can see our breath!" I puffed, and she wagged. The streets looked deserted and the quiet felt almost eerie. "Let's run!" I said to her, and we jogged toward the variety store. Seeing Beauty running alongside me again made me feel great.

Then suddenly she pulled to one side and barked as though she had to tell me something important—had to *yell* it, actually.

"What now? I didn't hear anything." Beauty bolted forward, yanking my arm from its socket. "Stop it, Beauty. You can't be a guide dog if you act like this." Still she plowed ahead.

That's when I saw where she was heading. Some clothes lay stretched near the sidewalk—so dark I would have never spotted them. She dragged me toward them. "That's funny. Why would anybody leave their clothes by the curb like that?"

Then I saw the clothes more clearly and gasped. "Oh, god, Beauty—it's a body!"

Kyle

Semiconscious

Aw, man, I'm freezing. I want to reach for the covers to pull them up over my head, but my arms feel like cement boulders. I can't even wiggle my fingers. The mattress against my back presses up cold and hard, like rock or—wait a minute—pavement! Where am I? Just as I think that thought, it floats away, and I can't remember why I feel so worried, only that I do. An electric current inside my gut circles around and around, making me want to run, jump and scream. I want to do something, but I can't remember what.

Stand up. That's it. I will my legs to bend and my feet to support me, but nothing moves. Now I want to get up so bad, I feel my body actually lift and float in the darkness.

Cold…I shiver. Where are my blankets? Why is my bed so hard?
RAWF!

A dog—no! I have to be dreaming. That's it, I'm really in my bed. I hear the panting and I'm little again. Five years old, and the same height as the Parkinses' dog. It's OK, you can pat Max. *That's what Mrs. Parkins always told me. But I am alone outside, on the front lawn; waiting, waiting for someone—Mom, maybe—and I have a cookie in my hand. The German shepherd runs toward me, long pink tongue hanging to one side. I back away but he jumps on me, his black nails digging into my arms.* Max loves children. He wouldn't hurt a fly, *Mrs. Parkins had said.*

I fall back. The cold pavement hits my back, hard. Hawh, hawh— the dog's panting is loud in my ears. It's all I can hear now. I can smell Max's meaty bad breath, but he's wagging his tail. He snaps up my cookie, nipping my fingers at the same time. Ow! I call, and I jerk my hand away. Then Max changes. I see his jaws drop open now, see his lips lift. His pant-ing turns to a snarl and his teeth into angry knives jabbing into my cheek.

I want to push him off, but I can't. I scream and scream for my mother. Instead, Mrs. Parkins rushes out and pulls Max away.

Were you teasing Max? You bad boy! *And then we're someplace else and it's so dark. I can't see anything. I hear panting and yipping, and then I feel it. Max's hot breath on my leg, Max's dagger teeth biting my ankle.* Isn't he a cute puppy? *Maddie's voice.*

But this is all wrong. Mom came out, we went to the doctor. I got stitches. It wasn't so dark. Why is it so dark?

Another thought filters through to me. It has to be a dream, because I can't see Max anymore. I'm blind. My teeth chatter. It's freezing. If it's a dream, why am I on the ground? And I hear panting, I really do.

My cheek feels wet. Is it blood?

There's a tongue lapping at my cheek. Ugh, I want to push it away but then Max will bite me. I can't see anything again, but I still feel the heaviness on my chest. Is this still a dream? The heaviness is warm and somehow comforting. In my mind I see it as an intense white light heating the chill out of my bones. It guides and focuses me. The ground, cold and hard against my back, can't hurt me—not while this anchor of heat weighs down on my chest. I can't be scared while I have this light. I reach to touch it.

Fur? No, it can't be Max. Max hates me. I'm a bad boy. I teased Max.

I hear a girl's voice in the distance—the girl from the park. The one who cried for me when Maddie broke off with me. Cry for me again, why don't you? My head hurts. Stay! *she calls.* I'll get help.

The dream must be over. I don't feel pain in the skin on my face. But my head still pounds behind my eyes and I float, even with that warm white light anchoring my chest down. Floating, floating…sirens wail in another dream, somewhere else. The weight springs off. Lifting, floating, shouts, floating. Nothing.

I imagine Max off my chest, teeth gleaming. I hand him my cookie this time. He looks happy. He doesn't bite me; he licks my face. This time no one stops him. More floating. If only this darkness could end.

Someone laughed in another room. Like silver bells. It was her—I was sure of it. I sat up quickly and felt a tube brush up against my arm.

"Careful, Kyle, you'll pull the IV out of your arm." Mom's voice?

"What IV? Where am I?" I sat up against softness. The smell of sickly-sweet medicine combined with that of deodorized blankets. I couldn't be in my room.

I heard the girl's voice again, from a distance. "Settle, Beauty. He's OK. We're going to go visit him." Then jingling.

"Mom, who is that? Outside my door. The dog!" Electricity snapped and crackled inside me, circling, making me want to jump up and run.

"Calm down, Kyle. You're in the hospital. Do you have any idea what happened?"

"A dog attacked me. He bit my face and then wouldn't get off. I hear him outside the door, Mom."

"Shh, shh. A girl and her dog found you in the street. You'd collapsed—had a hypo."

That voice. *Stay! I'll get help*. "The girl from the park?"
I thought out loud. *Jingle, jingle*. Was I imagining that
sound now?

"Well, lucky the girl knew you. She told the ambulance attendant you were diabetic. He thought you might
have just been drunk."

"I swear a dog attacked me."

"You must have been hallucinating. They're moni-
toring your blood sugar levels. They had to do an emergency infusion to bring your glucose levels back up."

*Max's hot panting on my face...his teeth bared, ready to sink on my
cheek...* "She let that dog bite me. She thought he was
friendly."

"Nothing like that happened." Her voice again.
Click, click—the sound of long black dog nails on the
linoleum.

"Oh, hello. Are you the girl who found my son?"

"I'm Elizabeth Kerr, and this is my dog Beauty."
The voice came closer. "I never let her bite Kyle. I told
her to stay while I went for help."

"Can't you see the scar?" I touched my cheek where
I knew it would be. "I needed ten stitches."

"Kyle, that was from Max. When you were little,"
Mom's hand touched my arm as she talked. "It was freezing out. Beauty kept you warm till the ambulance came."

My head pounded and thoughts collided together,
confusing me. That anchor of heat and light that had
focused me—I had touched it and it had felt *furry*. "But a

dog hurt me," I said, touching my scar again and feeling all mixed up. What was a dream; what was real?

"You're a liar!" the voice snapped out. "Come on, Beauty." The voice moved away.

"Wait!" I called as I swung my legs out from under my covers. That light that guided me, a dog? I wanted to know.

"Kyle, you can't upset yourself like this." Mom grabbed my legs and held them. "Lie down and rest."

The effort took too much out of me. I couldn't fight her.

Someone else came in then, fiddled with my IV, said hello and chatted us up—a nurse? "Did you see that chocolate Lab? What a beautiful dog. Wearing one of those green jackets. Training to be a guide dog, you know. You should really see about getting a dog like hers. You'd never have to walk alone."

CHAPTER 9

Elizabeth and Beauty

The Hospital Visit

My worst nightmare: a body on the ground with only me in the whole world responsible for it. I didn't want to be the one to check if it was dead or alive. I wanted to be sick, or run, or both. Here's where Beauty calmed *me* down, for a change, and helped me out.

She whined softly as she stepped closer to the guy, and I couldn't help watching her as she sniffed him over. He looked familiar and yet not. I mean, for me it's the eyes that really make a person, and obviously, this guy's were closed. Beauty sniffed closer to his neck and mouth, and then licked across his face.

"Is he breathing, girl?" I asked as I kneeled down. That's when I saw the sunglasses. Dark gelled hair, black jeans and a long-sleeved dark T. No one wore dark glasses when it was this dark; it had to be the blind guy from school. Beauty looked at me, shifted from paw to paw and whimpered.

He wasn't just a body, he was a person. I could do this now. I touched his neck and felt a pulse. Closer, and I even saw his chest rise. Alive! I wanted to tear around in circles till I figured out what to do.

"Stay!" I held up my hands like stop signs to Beauty. "Stay here, while I get help."

I didn't look back as I flew to the convenience store. "Call 911!" I yelled at the clerk. "There's a man hurt on the corner of Mountainside and Nottingham."

The clerk made me speak to the emergency operator, and I felt like I had repeated everything a hundred times before I ran back to the corner of the street.

Beauty lay half on top of Kyle's chest, haunches resting on the ground. Her eyes looked into mine as if to tell me this boy was all right, she was protecting him as best she could. Oh, my gosh, what would happen if a bus drove by? Nothing. I was sure by the way her head rested between those protective paws. Nothing would get between her and this human. Her tail flapped only once in greeting.

I started unsnapping my jacket, thinking, *Beauty has the right idea. We have to keep Kyle warm.* But then the ambulance warbled in the distance. A red light pulsed across Kyle's face.

Two attendants slammed down a stretcher. "On three," one told the other. "One, two and three." They hoisted him onto the stretcher. "How long has he been like this?" he asked as they lifted him into the back.

"I don't know. My dog found him as we were walking."

"Any ID?"

"I didn't check. But he goes to my school. Kyle
Nicholson. And my friend told me he's diabetic."

The guy nodded and talked to the other attendant.
Then they banged the doors shut and jumped into the
front.

"Where—where are you taking him?" I asked.

"Emergency at Joseph Brant. Thank you, miss."

"Elizabeth. I can call to see how he is, right?"

"Yes. Call the hospital."

Like the end of a bad dream, the ambulance pulled
away, wailing in inhales and exhales.

I walked home with Beauty, stunned. The sun magically
rose, brightening the sky with lighter and lighter shades of
gold, then yellow and then white—just as though nothing
was wrong. I stepped through the door and heard the shower going. Deb was up already?

She came down, sipping from a glass of water. "My
third glass," she told me. "I have to drink at least five before
the ultrasound. You haven't forgotten, have you? You're
still coming, aren't you?"

I bounced my palm on my forehead. "Ultrasound! Oh,
my gosh. I did forget. You'll never believe this, but…"

I told her all about finding Kyle. Beauty wolfed down
pieces of toast as I described the way she had lain across him
to keep him warm.

"Well, you can drop by on him. The ultrasound clinic is
in the basement of Joseph Brant."

"You're right. I can check. Oh, I hope he's OK." I

looked at Beauty. I didn't want to find out any bad news. If only Beauty could go in first and check, as she had earlier that morning.

Deb didn't mind that I was taking Beauty to the clinic.

"You should have seen how great she was with Kyle. She will make someone the perfect guide dog, if only she can get over her thing with buses and jackhammers."

"She'll do just fine. Just bring the Elvis tape," Debra reassured me. "Although I'm not sure how *I'm* going to do, with all this water sloshing inside me."

After everything that had happened, I thought that Debra had to be right about Beauty. So I was shocked when she backed up against me instead of heading up the bus steps.

"Come on, come on. Don't have all day," the bus driver said. "You gonna bring that dog in, at least shut the radio off," he told us.

No Elvis. We sat down in a middle seat. Deb didn't think she could take all the bumps in the back, not after five glasses of water. "Don't worry," she told me as Beauty circled her a third time before settling. "We'll sing lullabies. What's the driver gonna do? *Hushaby, hushaby. Baby, sleep,*" Deb crooned.

I sang along softly. It sounded calm, like a happy memory. I sighed. Beauty settled. "Hey, Deb? Did you ever have to sing this to me when I was a baby?"

"Uh-huh, always. I used to have to play with you to shut you up so Mom could study."

"Wow. Now I'll get to sing it to your baby." I started humming the tune again.

Twenty blocks later, I had to nudge Beauty awake with my foot as the bus rolled up to our stop. Beauty stepped down much quicker than she had climbed on. "We'll catch up to you at the elevator," I told Deb. Then Beauty and I ran together to the admissions desk. I asked about Kyle and the receptionist gave me his room number, so at least that meant he wasn't dead.

We rushed back to Debra, standing cross-legged at the elevators. Down we went to the clinic, where we had to wait in line at the counter just to check in and fill out forms. When she'd completed them, Debra still had to wait. "Ohhhh, I have to go," she moaned as she squeezed her eyes together. After fifteen minutes, she turned really pale and rushed to the counter a second time. Then she ran for the bathroom.

When she came back she looked a bit better, and just as she sat down, her name was called. She started after the technician but called back to me, "Coming?"

Beauty at my heels, I followed, feeling a little queasy about the whole thing. What did they do for an ultrasound, anyway? Would it hurt? Would I see blood and gory stuff?

Turned out I saw a white-and-gray blob, floating and pulsing on the screen. The technician first rubbed some gel onto Deb's slightly rounder tummy, and then rolled a giant-size computer mouse over it, illuminating various parts of the blob.

"There's its head," the technician said. I squinted, but Deb went gaga.

"Oh, look, Liz, it has a head already!"

"There's the umbilical cord, the legs…"

Somehow the technician turned up the volume on the baby's heartbeat and I heard this strange, alien *whomp-whoosh* over everything. Beauty's ears lifted, and she angled her head as if to listen closer. On inspiration, I turned on my tape machine. *Whomp-whoosh* and Elvis—what could be better for Beauty?

I tried to be as excited as Debra about the floating blob. "It looks just like you," I said, and instead of chucking me on the shoulder and laughing, Debra just beamed.

Then, after another trip to the bathroom, she joined Beauty and me as we tracked down Kyle's room, up on the third floor. I didn't know whether I could just walk in. I was about to rap my knuckles on the open door, but I saw someone was already with him, so I hesitated. I didn't mean to eavesdrop, but I heard snatches of what Kyle said to the lady sitting beside him. *What?* He said Beauty had attacked him. *No!*

He even talked about stitches and no one coming to help him. I marched in there to confront him. *Liar!*

His mom—the lady beside him—tried to smooth things over. But she couldn't smooth over the fact that her son was a jerk. I pulled Beauty back sharply so she wouldn't get blamed for anything else, and we left.

"Come on, Debra. A guy like that deserves to be stuck with a white cane the rest of his life."

Kyle

The Support Group

I fell back asleep, so deathly tired, I didn't think I could ever bring myself to wake up again. But then I sensed someone's presence near me. I tried to ignore it, but there was something else I wanted to do, somebody else I wanted to chase after. It was urgent, but I couldn't catch hold of the thought fully.

"Ahem." A polite cough and the sound of a tapping pen against a notebook, or bulletin board, made me sit up.

"It's Dr. Peters here." *The diabetes specialist, of course.* "I just want to go over what happened to you." He re-explained what Mom had already told me: how my blood sugar had dropped and I'd nearly gone into a diabetic coma.

"Sometimes this happens when you sleep in, exercise, miss a meal..."

Or get hammered. Except I didn't exactly want to tell him about the drinking, especially not with Mom sitting there, listening.

"You know, here at the hospital there's a really good diabetes support group for teens. They meet once a month, and even get together for other social events. Makes everyone feel better to know there are others in the same boat."

Others in the same boat. "Is there anyone else there who's blind?"

Silence, dead silence.

"I didn't think so. Listen, I think you should know that I went to a party last night and got drunk. Otherwise, this wouldn't have happened at all."

Mom gasped.

"I see," Dr. Peters said, and then went into a spiel about the perils of alcohol and diabetes; the sharp ups and downs in blood sugar that excessive drinking caused.

"I won't drink anymore," I told him wearily. Who wanted to hear more lectures?

"You don't have to swear off parties for life. Just pay attention to your body signals and your Glucometer. Listen, why don't you try the support group? They'll give you tips on drinking responsibly and staying in control. Good control is everything with diabetes."

Control—what a laugh. "Thank you, Doctor. I'll work harder at it," I told him.

"Well, you can probably go home tomorrow morning, then, if all things stay the same." Dr. Peters clapped his hand on my shoulder. "Take care, Kyle. And let me know if you change your mind about the group."

Mom started in on me the moment he left. She was obviously really keen on the idea. "Come on, Kyle. If these teens have a party, everything there would be dietetic. You could relax and not worry so much about what to eat, at the very least…"

She wouldn't have to worry so much about what I ate.

Dad and Shawna came to visit next. Dad immediately joined the campaign for the teen support group. "Now, why wouldn't you want to join that?" he asked.

Why couldn't they all just leave it alone? And to top it all off, Shawna also had another plan to shove down my throat, whether I wanted it or not. I heard Dad's laptop beep as it powered up.

"What's that?" I asked.

"Just listen," Shawna said, and I heard a diskette click into the drive. "This is information on the guide dog program."

She and Dad *oohed* and *aahed* as this voice explained the program along with all the requirements.

"Who would look after the dog?" Mom asked a few minutes later, when the voice stopped.

"Well, Kyle would have it with him all day, like the man said. Even at school," Shawna said in an amazed, happy tone. "But then after, at home, when he takes the dog's harness off, it could be everybody's."

"You mean *yours*," I pointed out. It was that amazed, happy tone that got to me. My blindness would turn into her greatest wish come true.

"Sounds like another great ah-dea," Dad drawled.

"Oh, come on," Mom interrupted. "Kyle's hated

dogs ever since the Parkinses' German shepherd bit him."

"It has nothing to do with that!" But in my mind I heard Max's rumbling growl. I tried to think, instead, of that warm weight on my chest last night. *Beauty stayed with you and kept you warm.* I saw again the bright light in my mind—brighter than any night-light, guiding. I tried to combine that vision of light and sensation of heaviness with the touch of fur.

That was the urgent thing I still needed to do. I should tell that girl from the park that I had been dreaming and mixed up; that I was sorry I had accused her dog of biting me. I fingered the scar on my cheek.

"Well, if he's not afraid of dogs anymore, ah say let's fill out those forms we got," my father said.

"What?" my mother and I both said at the same time.

"Well, Mother, you said so yourself. That girl's Lab found our boy last night. Saved him, really."

"But you didn't know that when you sent away for those forms," Mom said.

"I did it. I was the one," Shawna piped up. "You know, after that show. I checked out the Web sites and e-mailed four schools for more information."

I clicked my tongue in disgust and shook my head.

A moment's pause. "Well, it wasn't like you were going to do anything on your own. You never do, anymore," Shawna continued.

"Look, Kyle, these things take a lawng time, anyways," Dad drawled. "Like it said on the CD, we need to get a report from your school, a recommendation from your O & M instructor, some references…. Why don't you just let Shawna and me help you with these forms. If the school accepts you and you still don't like the idea, well…"

A recommendation from my O & M workers—that should nix their plan nicely. How many times have I let both Jack and Amber know that I have a dog phobia? I sighed and wished I didn't. Last night—well, actually, early this morning, what had really happened? I replayed all the sensations. I tried really hard in my mind to focus on the light, the warmth and the weight on my chest; those weren't so bad after all. Then I remembered again the feel of the lapping tongue on my face and the fur under my fingers. I tried not to tense up. From somewhere I recalled the good sounds: the laughing girl from the park talking in the hospital earlier, the dog collar jingling. Couldn't I make myself want a dog like that? But then I heard Max's growling in my mind, felt his gouging black nails, imagined his snapping jaws. Ugh, what was the use? I knew I just could not trust a dog.

"Go ahead, fill out the forms. They'll never accept me, anyway," I said.

"And will you join that group?" Dad pushed on. "Probably if you'd gone to a meeting earlier, you would have known how to correctly compensate for the extra alcohol you consumed last night. You wouldn't have needed a dawg to save you."

I shook my head and sighed. "Did it ever occur to any of you that we would have all been better off had I not been saved?"

CHAPTER 10

Elizabeth and Beauty

Trial by Audio Tape

So Beauty wasn't appreciated by one dysfunctional blind guy. Who cared, right? It's just that when it was time to give her up, I wanted to picture someone truly worthy, not Kyle. Still, I tried not to be in a bad mood, for Debra's sake. The ultrasound had made her so happy. "I really am having a baby!" she said. "Play the heartbeat again!"

Whomp-whoosh, whomp- whoosh. Beauty settled nicely on the bus, listening to it, and back home it seemed to have a magical effect on everyone too.

"A nice, healthy heartbeat," Dad said when I played it at supper.

Mom still looked as though she wanted to waken from a bad dream when anything to do with the baby was mentioned. But the lines on her face seemed to soften and smooth at that sound. *Whomp-whoosh, whomp-whoosh*. "When is your next appointment with the doctor?"

"Monday at ten," Debra answered.

"I have a free period at that time. I can take you."

What a breakthrough for Mom. I looked for a reaction from Deb. None; she just ate her lentils and spinach quietly. Lots of calcium and protein in that meal. No one bugged her to eat meat or drink milk today.

"Hey, I only have ten more quarterly reviews to do," Dad offered brightly—his idea of good news.

"But aren't those all for last quarter?" I asked as I picked up one of Mom's famous barbecue ribs.

Wrong thing to say. I could tell right away, by the way Dad's face kind of froze. "Yes, that's true. I'll have to at least get a couple of projects launched before I can evaluate them with my own notes."

"Mmm. You'll manage. You always do," Mom told him.

"Well, I feel fabulous." Debra waved her fork in the air. "Alive and creative. I think I'm going to rip up my old painting and do an entire retake of *Camel on a Surfboard* after supper. How is your suite of poems coming, Mother?" Debra smiled, a piece of spinach dangling from her front teeth.

The lines all tightened up across Mom's face again. "I have the worst writer's block ever," she grumbled. "I should be able to write two poems in my sleep."

"Rip up all the old stuff. I say start fresh," Debra suggested, flinging her arms wide, cutlery still in hand.

I signaled with a rib bone to my teeth so Deb would get the spinach out.

"Play the baby's heartbeat again," she said, instead. *Whomp-whoosh, whomp-whoosh.* Beauty came over, attracted either by the sound or the way I waved the rib in front of my face.

"Maybe I'll just do that," Mom said, breaking into a surprised smile. "I can't get into the mindset of those others. And I have time to write a new suite, after all."

"And you're a far better writer now than you've ever been," Debra added, spinach-free now. Perhaps finally she was acknowledging Mom's breakthrough on baby doctor appointments.

"Can I cut some of the meat off these bones and give them to Beauty?" I asked, interrupting their moment. "She was the best dog in the universe on the bus and in the hospital."

"Take those three from the pan on the stove," Mom said. "Oh—which reminds me: Scott called. Says he found a road repair site and taped the sound of the jackhammer for you."

"Wow, that was so thoughtful of him. I'll call him right after I feed Beauty." I cut off some meat into Beauty's dish and made her wait the ten-second countdown. At the word go she chowed down on the dog-and-people-food blend with such gusto, I felt pretty sure her depression was cured, if not her noise phobia.

Meanwhile, I grabbed the portable and dialed Scott's number. The line buzzed in short pulses. Busy. *Sigh.* I called again twice later—no answer—and the third time left a message. "Well, I'll see him at school tomorrow, Beauty. Maybe he'll give me the tape then."

Next day I did catch a glimpse of him, on the bleachers with Gwen, but he wouldn't have noticed me. He was too busy, "sucking up her lungs," as Alicia put it.

Alicia put her hand on my shoulder. "I *know* he still likes you. I don't get this thing with Gwen at all."

Which made two of us.

I was ready to give up totally until he just showed up at our house Friday night, tape in hand. I tried not to smile too hard, or let everything inside me rise up to greet him. Friday night is prime date time, after all. But Beauty wagged all my feelings openly.

"Here are the sound effects. But…" Scott grinned with excitement, "I just noticed they're digging up the street on Mapleview. If we hurry, we can test Beauty on the live jack-hammer sound, complete with vibrating ground effects."

"All right! Just give me a sec." I snatched up the tape player from the shelf in the family room, grabbed a jacket and snapped on Beauty's leash. "I'm going for a walk," I hollered back through the house. I knew that Mom was writing at the computer in the basement and Dad was pounding nails into wallboard for the baby's room, which guaranteed nobody heard me. Beauty didn't even jump a the sound of Dad's hammering. Good stuff. I slammed the door happily behind us.

We jogged to get to the construction site more quickly. Beauty always enjoyed a good run. By the time we got to

Mapleview, though, the workers had all gone home. "We can try out the audio tape on her, anyway," Scott said as we strolled, more slowly now, along the dug-up pavement.

"Wait, I want you to hear this first." I pressed the *Play* button. *Whomp-whoosh, whomp-whoosh.* Beauty lifted her ears slightly as she picked her way through the broken asphalt.

My hand brushed up against Scott's, and my whole arm tingled.

"What is that?" Scott asked.

"My sister's baby's heartbeat. Cool, huh?" I tried. But the magic didn't seem to work on him.

"I guess. It sounds like lots of liquid sloshing around." We turned to head back and I bumped into him. He held me steady so I wouldn't topple. *Whomp-whoosh, whomp-whoosh*—my heart beat almost as fast as the baby's, but then he let me go.

I couldn't make my heart slow down again, so I finally exchanged the baby tape for the one of the jackhammer. I turned it up as loud as possible but it just didn't sound as threatening as it had that day when we stepped off the bus. Beauty tilted her head to an angle and gave me her golden stare.

"Maybe she's really cured." Scott smiled at me, the paleness around his mouth signaling the start of one of his blushes.

I wanted to be cured too, so I turned away and we continued home. When we got back to my front door, I faced him again.

"Thanks, Scott, for helping me with Beauty."

I went to kiss his cheek—just a friendly thank-you kiss—but as I drew closer, I changed my mind and kissed his lips. He grabbed my elbow and continued the kiss. Finally when we broke apart, he shook his head. "Oh, man, what you do to me."

I looked him straight in the eye and waited for him to say something. To tell me that it was all over with Gwen, that he wanted to go out with me from now on. Instead he shook his head again, turned and walked away.

Kyle

O & M with Maddie

We'd all be better off if I was dead. That's what I was really saying, and no one would ever admit to that. Instead Mom was ticked off.

"How could you say such a thing!" She was also ticked that I wouldn't change my mind about the support group. "With your attitude, I'm not sure you even want to help yourself."

Maybe she was right. Apart from the hallucinations of Max, it had been comfortable floating around, dreaming. Death didn't seem so bad, and there had been that warmth and light. It was life that seemed like hell.

Dad really needed all his time to prepare for his big trial, so anything that pleased Mom and kept her quiet would have been good about now, a teen support group included. I almost felt sorry for him—especially when Mom announced her "really exciting news" over artificially sweetened pudding that night.

"I know you'll all be happy to hear I've finally made the Automotive All-Star team. I'll be meeting with the rest of the nominees for a celebration and strategy exchange from Wednesday through the weekend."

"In my trial week?" Dad asked.

"I was hoping you'd drive Kyle to and from school."

"Why can't we just call Jack and get him to show Kyle how to do it on his own? Kyle's a big boy, and this isn't going to go away."

"No time. And I don't want to worry. For once in my life, when I finally make the list—in a year with a sales slump, too—I think I deserve to go away without having to worry."

"Ah go to court next week. Don't you understand? Ah can't just walk out in the middle of a trial to act as chauffeur."

"Why can't Shawna walk me?" I suggested.

"Nobody walks with their big brother," Shawna answered. "And you'd make me late. I start at eight, remember?"

"I'll just have to cancel my trip," Mom said.

"Don't cancel!" I slammed my hand down on the table, making the cutlery clink. "And don't worry! This is *my* problem. I can solve it." I pushed myself away and

stood up. "I'll call a friend." Great plan, but I couldn't
even find the portable alone. I stumbled and groped
through the house, following the pager beep, until finally Shawna just handed it to me. Then I called Rebecca
and Sarah, who both had dance committee and soccer
practice before and after school.

"Call Maddie. You know you still love her," Shawna
suggested.

"Shut up," I answered. Instead I dialed the last person anyone would want to rely on, and asked him.

"Hey, man, no problem," Ryan answered. "But
you're missing your chance, dude. If you want to get
back in with Maddie, ask her. Tell her she's the only one
who can do it. While you're at it, tell her you want to feel
her face. Who knows where that could lead to?"

I gritted my teeth and silently counted to ten. I
didn't want to say anything to blow my only escort,
sleazemaster or not. "Wednesday morning, then, eight-
fifteen?" I said.

"Absolutely." The phone clicked off at the other
end.

Mom seemed even less thrilled with the arrangement
than I was. "We don't know this boy, or his parents."

"I'm not going to marry him, Mom."

Dad cracked up over that one. "Come awn. He's
going to school with a buddy. What could be more normal than that? He should be walking every day. A little
fresh air can't hurt him."

The *normal* and the *fresh air* bits got me—like I was
some kind of invalid. And then on Wednesday, Ryan
drifted by at eight-thirty. We ended up twenty minutes
late, since he needed a smoke before he went in.

It was Ryan's third late that month; my second, so
only he earned a detention. But I might as well have gotten one too, since I had to stay behind and wait for him.
That's when, it seemed, fate took over.

I'd told Ryan I'd wait for him in the resource center, planning to listen to *A Separate Peace* and get the jump
on my English assignment. Most of the kids had left for
the day, and without three hundred teeming bodies, the
O & M stuff Jack had shown me worked a little better. I
could hear voices, follow the sound of a computer game
coming from the lab. As I *tap-swished* my way through the
halls, I suddenly smelled tangerine and heard keys jan-
gling.

"I've got the car today. Do you want a ride home?"
Maddie asked.

I hesitated, willing myself to say no. *Have some pride*, I
thought, but I suddenly just missed her so badly.
"Thanks, I'd really like that."

"Do you want to take my arm?"

I folded the cane away and gratefully wrapped my
fingers around the warmth of her upper arm.

She asked me how I was doing and why I was still
hanging around so late, and I told her about Mom's
sales conference.

"That is a really big deal for her, isn't it? Do you want me to ask my Mom if I can use the car for the rest of the week? I'm sure she'd understand."

I thought for a moment. That would have been so easy, but I wanted Maddie to see me as more than someone just needing a lift. I also wanted to show Dad I could manage without some stupid dog.

"I have a bigger favor to ask you. The O & M instructors are always so backlogged. Could you just come with me back and forth to school a couple of times? I want to be able to do it myself."

I couldn't watch her face to see why Maddie hesitated, but I held my breath. Those few moments of silence meant she had to at least have been thinking about it. If she agreed, it also had to mean something, didn't it? Absurdly, I did want to run my fingers over her face—to feel whether her brow was furrowed, her eyebrows up or calmly down. Her mouth pursed or smiling.

"I can't do it right now. I promised Mom I'd pick up the groceries for her."

She wouldn't get off that easy. "I meant tomorrow and the next day, to school and back."

She hesitated. "Sure. Why don't I come by early, say eight o'clock, and we'll head over on the bus together?"

"Thanks, Maddie." She guided me into the car and we chatted the rest of the way about ordinary things. Like our English assignment, and how we both thought we had to pretend John Knowles's book really appealed to

us, to get a better mark. And what we were going to do
with our lives. Maddie wanted to go into medicine. Did I
still want to go into law?

"I don't know. Maybe music. Dad once said eye
contact with clients is really important."

"Aw, parents say dumb stuff they don't really mean."

She turned the car then, and stopped the engine.
"See you tomorrow."

I waited for a moment. "Yeah, sure. That would be
great, Maddie." I slid out of the car and shut the door. I
walked, smooth and steady, up to my own door, not
bothering with the cane. I even whistled as I headed to
my room to listen to *A Separate Peace*.

Maddie doesn't identify with the character either, I thought as I
typed up my response journal. Maddie, Maddie,
Maddie. Light filled up my whole soul. Tomorrow I
would be with her; she would count blocks with me, and
steps. I couldn't even understand or name the secret
hope that was building with all that light.

It kept building the next morning. Five blocks of
walking; knowing beautiful Maddie, with the slightly
upturned nose, was following. I didn't fear for my life as
I listened for traffic and confidently stepped off the
curbs. I never swerved on the sidewalk nor missed a step
as I climbed onto the bus. After school she came home
with me, too. It felt so good, like nothing had changed
between us. Friday would be our last two walks together,
so I planned once again to ask her to a party at Ryan's.

Instead I was shocked when she introduced Adam at the end of the day. "Adam's going to meet me at your house so we can go out after. Or did you just want a lift home?"

"No!" I snapped, my stomach tightening into a fist. "I need the practice." We got on the bus together silently, everything inside me dropping and darkening. I asked the driver to announce my stop and found us a seat. I decided I had to at least try again. "Maddie, I really wanted you to come to Ryan's with me."

"Oh, right, I'm supposed to help you get to the Coma Palace. It's two stops after school. I'm sure he can send someone to meet you."

"No, you don't understand. I wanted you there with me."

"You just met Adam." She sighed. "You have to know I only want to be your friend."

Then I became too desperate. I reached for her face and leaned toward it, forcing a kiss on her. She didn't return it. Instead she pushed me away.

"I can't stand it, Maddie. I can't just be friends."

"That is your problem!"

"Sunnydale Avenue!" the bus driver called, and I stood shakily. I shuffled off, with Maddie following, and when she got into Adam's car I couldn't even tell her goodbye. I didn't trust my voice.

It still cracked and rasped when I picked up the ringing phone ten minutes later.

"Ready to go for a beer run?" Ryan asked.

"I don't know." Did it sound like I'd been crying? "Maddie just pulled away with her boyfriend."

"Aw, man. What a bummer." He waited for a few seconds. "Tell you what. Let's get the beer. Then we'll take the top down and you can take the Mustang for a spin. Just to make things interesting, you can back it around the parking lot this time."

CHAPTER 11

Elizabeth and Beauty

Cloud Shapes

Friday night, and Scott had spent it with me. Most people would wonder about that. I mean, maybe he'd even had a fight with Gwen. Maybe he was free to take me to the semi-formal coming up in a few weeks—that's what Alicia had suggested, anyway. I should buzz right up to him and invite him out before they had a chance to make up.

Just lucky I went to the bathroom at the right time to hear about Rebecca's karaoke sleepover. Apparently Gwen did a great Britney Spears imitation.

So Scott had spent time with me only because Gwen had been busy. I could have made such a fool of myself. Still, Alicia begged me to come to the dance anyway. She wanted to go, and I looked so great dressed up. I needed to show Scott that I could have a great time without him.

The dance was in three weeks—the Friday of Beauty's final assessment, actually. But there were posters all over, announcements almost every day, pushing buying tickets in advance to save a couple of bucks. Alicia bought us a pair, convinced she could change my mind. I talked to Deb and she pulled out a really cute black two-piece leather outfit. Beauty sniffed it approvingly.

"I'm not going to fit into this for a while. You can borrow it," she said as she held it against me.

"But should I go, Deb?" Beauty sat down, tongue hanging out, waiting for my decision.

"Of course! Have a good time! How does that country song go, that Dad always plays? 'Better to be sorry for something you've done than for something you've never tried.'"

"Yeah, but Scott only spends time with me when Gwen's busy." Beauty sank down, head between her paws.

"Did you ever think you might only find Scott attractive because of Gwen? I mean, you told me last year when you broke up, the feeling was mutual."

"No." I slipped the leather jacket over my T-shirt and looked at myself in the mirror.

"Remember, you only noticed Scott after Alicia went out with him."

"But I haven't gone out with another guy since," I complained as I shimmied out of jeans and slipped on the skirt. "Alicia's gone out with four."

"So you're pickier. When you least expect to meet someone new, there he will be, the perfect one. Ooh, that black leather works on you."

"Yeah! I really like it." So I decided to go. Beauty

scrambled up, sniffed again and wagged her tail. I must have smelled like a giant rawhide treat to her.

Alicia and I spent some time in the mall buying accessories: purple beads, and earrings. Beauty came with me. Of course, there wasn't much time to make really sure she behaved well on the bus. We hummed to her and she stopped pacing. I thought she should do OK on her tests.

I didn't trust Deb's platforms so I borrowed some short black boots from Alicia. Everything looked so great together, I knew that Friday would go perfect. But when I got home that Friday afternoon, Beauty's assessment day, she wasn't in her crate yet. Had she flunked? Mom wasn't around to ask. I dressed and ate some microwavable pizza, waiting and wondering.

She never showed up, either, and I had to leave for the dance. None of Alicia's compliments made me feel any better as I stepped up to the dance table and handed in my ticket.

"Too bad they let the tweenies in," I heard someone say. Oh, no, not him! It was the blind guy, Kyle, and the other greasy senior who always ogled all the girls.

"Look, you two match," Alicia said, because of course, Kyle was dressed in his cool-dude blacks. "Gosh, he's cute," she added, and I couldn't lie enough to disagree. Alicia giggles when she's nervous, and sometimes it's catchy. I found myself laughing a lot that night. Even when I saw Scott and Gwen being separated by a teacher, they were so all over each other. Even when Alicia paired up with a guy from computer science. Even when the blind guy jammed along with the other guitarist in the band. He sang a solo, too, called "Too Many Girls for One Guy." He strutted and sang, so sure of himself, I didn't feel sorry for him at all, no matter what Scott said. After that number—and witnessing Gwen and Scott in the hall—I couldn't giggle anymore.

My mouth felt tired. I tried to call home about Beauty, but no one answered, so finally I snuck out and caught the first bus home.

"Beauty!...Beauty!" No dog rushed me at the door. I held my hand to my chest. She must have panicked at a sound. Then the trainer might have just kept her, to work on her himself.

"Mom! Deb!" I thought I heard soft, tinkling music coming from downstairs so I pounded down, calling, "Is anyone home?"

I followed the tinkling Brahms' Lullaby to the baby's room which—surprise, surprise—now had a door. I opened it, and the music-box chimes grew louder. A circle of bears danced from a white hook screwed to the side of a new white crib.

Mom lay on the shiny new wood floor beside the crib, scribbling madly on a yellow pad. When she finally looked up, her eyes seemed focused on a dream going on inside her head.

Beside her, Beauty, with her lip hooked over her incisor, wagged her butt.

"Hold still, girl, if you want me to get you right!" Deb

said from her spot on a stepladder. "Oh, hi, Liz." She pulled down a little paint mask from her nose. "How was the dance?"

"Fine," I answered, staring up at a fluffy white cloud Deb seemed to be shading in to look like a Labrador retriever. "How did Beauty do on her test?"

"No complaints, from what I heard," Mom answered. "What rhymes with Teal? So many things...zeal, squeal..." Mom continued, madly scribbling.

"Guess what!" Deb brightened and smiled, a new thing for my sister. Her whole face softened and warmed.

"What?"

"We had to have another ultrasound today. The doctor thought there was something off about the baby's due date."

"Uh-huh?"

"And his picture's over there on his new bureau!"

"His?" I stared at what looked like a huge negative with a vague, blobby outline of a baby.

"That's Teal's penis." Deb pointed with her paintbrush to another blob.

"Teal?" I asked.

"It's the color of the paint I used for the backdrop of the clouds. Mom thought it was a great word for her poem. I loved it too. Could be a girl's name, too, if the ultrasound is wrong."

"Baby Teal," I said out loud, still trying to get used to the idea and make the baby real to me. I wanted to make the name fit to the unknown gray blob, too. I wound up the

circle of bears and then lay down on the floor between
Mom and Beauty, staring up at those clouds, listening to
the lullaby.

Debra had shaded them all in differently so that you
could pick out suggestions of animals. "That's you right
there, Beauty!" I pointed up to the dog cloud Deb had just
finished. Beauty lifted her head up and then, looking confused, just licked my face. "You won't be here when the
baby comes. But I'll show him, and whenever I look up at
that cloud, I'll remember you."

Kyle

Hit!

Even after Mom returned from her conference, I fought
with her to continue getting to school on my own. "I
need to get around without you," I insisted. "And without constant practice, I lose my bearings." Dad support-
ed my stand, suggesting that maybe soon I'd get into the
guide-dog program and then she wouldn't have to worry
at all. *Fat chance*, I thought, feeling pretty safe from that.
Hopefully, by the time they realized I'd never be accepted into the guide-dog program, my new-found independence would have softened their disappointment.
Mom's and Dad's, at least—Shawna was really in it for
the dog.

Without Maddie in my life, I continued hanging

from the arm of any girl I could coax to Ryan's Coma Palace. They all liked the sad songs I wrote and sang, but I never could attach myself to anyone. It was like that one rap song always played in my head:

> *You think she'll always love you*
> *But her love might fade away.*

None of the girls seemed worth the risk. Not like Maddie.

Every other weekend, Ryan's parents would conveniently take off. And now at the beer store, I shuffled up to the cash on my own, instead of begging for help to buy a two-four. Either my sunglasses aged me or the clerk just couldn't bring himself to card a blind guy.

At the school semiformal in November, I met Andrea, whom I asked to Ryan's next party. She didn't have her license, though, and said she'd have to meet me there.

Mom and Dad weren't around to drive me either, although I hung around for a while, waiting. Finally I decided. By bus it was only two stops after school. Heck, I'd just ask the driver for help and go on my own.

Shawna freaked. "You can't leave. It's dark and practically blizzarding outside."

"Shawna, there's a girl waiting for me there. I can't stand her up, can I? Besides, what difference does it make to me whether it's dark or not?" There was nothing Shawna could say or do to keep me from going, and I left before she could try.

But I felt the cold snow sting my face the moment I stepped outside, and my feet skimmed over the silky surface of the sidewalk. "Go slow. Take it easy," I told myself. "No hurry. Andrea can wait a few extra minutes."

Clickety-clack. My cane sounded harsh and sharp against the soft *whoo, whoo* of the wind. First block, I stopped on the curb and listened as usual, but the wind blanketed all sound. I didn't hear any cars. Second block, I paused, inhaling deeply to calm myself down. My heart beat with the same *clickety-clack* rhythm as my stick as I forced myself to cross. A car tapped its horn to signal just as I reached what felt like the midpoint of the road. "Go ahead," someone called, maybe from a rolled-down car window. I continued across. Not so bad. There I was safe.

Then the last big-whammy intersection, the four-way stop. So everyone had to stop. No problem, right? I just had to lead with my identi-cane; all the drivers could see I was blind and wait patiently till I crossed.

I remembered what Amber had said about drivers watching for other cars instead of people. I also remembered Ryan nearly colliding with another car when he couldn't figure out who'd arrived first to the corner. "Ah, what the hell," he'd said and I'd felt him accelerate. I couldn't see how close we'd come, of course, but the screeching tires and his "Damn! Where did that baby carriage come from?" made me breathe a lot quicker.

Today I heard only the wind, so I paused for a few seconds and then headed across. Absolutely nothing happened. I'd made it across. This was so easy—after dark and in a storm. All that practice had paid off. I'd never be afraid of anything again. Just to the end of the block, about another sixty steps or so and I could wait for the bus. Ten, twenty, thirty...I'd counted out forty-five steps when a sound to my right froze me to the spot. An engine roared to life.

It happened in a split second. I yelled out too late. Wham! Hard metal slammed into my legs. A moment of pain, and then the force knocked me to the ground. The second impact blasted white pain like forks of lightning right up into my head.

The white seared at the back of my eyes, lighting all my thoughts up in a flash. And then, as always, everything turned dark again.

* * *

This was getting to be a habit, waking up in a hospital bed, a solid mass of ache. When I shifted, the pounding in my head made my eyes tear.

"Son? Can you hear me?" Dad called softly.

I tried to move my lips. They felt dry and cracked.

Mom spoke at me next. "You've been hit by a car, but you're all right."

I grabbed my head to stop the pounding and swirling.

"But I'd crossed the intersection. I wasn't even on the street."

"No, some idiot backed out of his driveway," Dad's voice boomed.

"Geez, my head is killing me."

"You have a concussion and some bruises, but otherwise you were really lucky." Mom's voice again.

"Lucky?" My hands trembled as I pulled them away from my head. I remembered the impact of the metal against my legs, the cement crashing into my head. My whole body shook as I felt the fear and pain all over again. "I got hit by a car on a sidewalk, Mom. Do you find that lucky?"

"Now son, snappin' at your mother right now's not gonna help anyone."

But I needed to snap at someone. I'd practiced and mastered walking by myself with that stupid cane. I'd stepped out into the streets trying to conquer my fears, and I'd done it. I should have been all right, but in the end nothing helped. I felt hot with frustration at my helplessness. Mom touched my brow with a cool, cool hand, and I pushed it away.

"I'm sorry about this, Kyle." Mom did sound as though she held herself responsible. "We shouldn't have gone out without making sure you had a ride."

"Yeah, we're sorry," Dad agreed. "You just can't go walking anywhere on your own. It's not safe."

"I can't have a life, really." The inside of my chest

started aching to match the rest of my body. "That driver might as well have killed me."

"Don't say that, Kyle. Please."

I couldn't talk anymore. It was hard enough to just swallow. A nurse came in and gave me some painkillers. My whole body turned into a cement block that sank to the bottom of a pool of darkness.

I dreamed I was dead. I couldn't move my fingers or toes, couldn't lift my arms or legs; my whole body was an anchor. But I could hear voices off in the distance: Shawna, Dad, Mom. I wanted to open my eyes and see them one more time. But oh, no, I caught a thought drifting in that blackness. *You're blind, Kyle. You can't see.*

Then could I hug Shawna and argue with my dad? Could I taste Mom's roasted chicken? Could I feel an icy wind numb my face in Ryan's Mustang? Could I smell Maddie's tangerine perfume, kiss her lips? Or any girl's? Another thought drifted in like a fluffy cloud. *No. You're dead, Kyle.* Nothing, no one. An eternity of this heaviness and emptiness.

"I don't want to be dead."

It wasn't even something that had come from my head; no drifting. The words just shot from my mouth. Once I'd said them I woke up, head still aching.

A gentle hand lay on top of mine. I could smell Maddie but I no longer trusted that scent. "Who's there?"

"It's me."

Then I *had* truly died. I let my head sink back into the pillow.

"Kyle, listen, I came as soon as I heard. I'm sorry." It was Maddie!

Another apology. "Oh, what for? You didn't back up over me."

"I didn't practice with you to Ryan's."

"That wouldn't have saved me. That last leg of the trip wouldn't have made a difference. The car hit me five blocks from home. You would have had to come with me all the way."

"That's what I mean. I should have come to Ryan's with you. Adam's not a boyfriend. I just asked him to go out that Friday so I couldn't change my mind."

I heard the catch in her voice. "About us?" I imagined her eyes shining with tears.

"About us."

"Well, you know what?" I took her hand and squeezed. "Don't blame yourself. You can't handle my blindness. I find it really hard myself."

"You don't understand. I'd like to try again, if you would too."

"What? Really? Oh, gosh, Maddie, sure."

She kissed me then. A slow, long kiss. I could hardly trust it. Maybe this was a dream, maybe I was in heaven. After a minute she spoke again. "I brought you a rose. An official going-out-again present. Smell?"

I felt a velvety tickle against my nostrils and inhaled

a flowery sweetness.

"I love the way the petals feel."

"Me too." I sneezed twice in a row. "Ow." I grabbed for my head again.

"Poor baby." Maddie chuckled and kissed my forehead. It was all too much for me and I suddenly felt I might cry. Not trusting myself, I lay back again, pretending to drift away into sleep. Maddie kissed my cheek and then no more tangerine Sunrise.

Oh, Maddie, I thought. And then I really did fall asleep. Not sinking to the bottom like last time. More like floating in a warm, comforting blackness. Floating, floating. *I don't want to be dead*, I told the darkness. *I can't be dead yet.*

"Kyle, Kyle, wake up." Someone shook my shoulder. "I'm so ticked off at you. I told you shouldn't go out when it was dark."

"Hi, Shawna, nice to see you, too."

"That's just it, Kyle. You think as long as you can't see anyone, it doesn't matter whether they can see you or not."

"Shawna, what are you talking about?"

"Going out after dark, stupid! It didn't make any difference to you, getting to Ryan's house. But for drivers, they can't see you in the darkness!"

"Oh, Shawna, my head. Leave me alone, will ya?"

"I can't leave you alone. You're always doing stupid stuff that lands you in the hospital. Everyone thinks you do it on purpose."

"On *purpose*, I got hit by a car?"

"Well, sure. You went out alone in a storm. And you drank too much when you knew what it could do to your blood sugar. And you wouldn't even think about joining the teen diabetes group."

I paused for a minute. "OK, OK, so I'll join the support group. Geez, anything to get you guys off my back. But listen, I have to do things on my own. *Have* to— do you understand? Even if everyone worries. Even though I'm afraid."

Shawna didn't say anything.

"Every time I step off a curb, Shawna, it's the scariest thing in the world. Scarier than…" I stopped for a moment, thinking, *It's scarier than facing a snarling German shepherd with bared fangs.* I tried a new thought on. Mom and Dad really believed I shouldn't go out alone. But I needed my independence, so the alternative was…but I'd blown that, hadn't I? With the O & M instructors, and with everyone, really, I'd been vocal and vehement about my attitude toward dogs. There wasn't anything I could do to change the past.

But I had to try. "Shawna, can you give me all the phone numbers of the guide-dog programs? I need to do some fast talking."

CHAPTER 12

Elizabeth and Beauty

January

Deb crossed the weeks and days off on the calendar, she was so anxious to have her baby. But I held myself back as I watched the calendar spaces fill. I didn't want time to pass too quickly, because Beauty was going back to Canine Vision on January fifteenth.

By New Year's, Debra was so huge that people kept asking her if she was carrying twins. If that didn't put her in a bad enough mood, at her January appointment the doctor told her to cut down on salt. She couldn't even pretend to enjoy her murky-green vegan meals anymore, so she became a full-fledged meatatarian again. Only she claimed *then* that normal food gave her headaches.

"Oh, come on," Mom said to that one. "Your dad eats a bacon-cheese double-meat patty and feels great. You need to get out more, get some fresh air."

So, even though it was freezing outside and Deb hated walking anywhere, she came with Beauty and me at least three times a day. January eleventh, twelfth, thirteenth, fourteenth. Not so much because of what Mom had said, but because but she wanted desperately to keep her weight down. Someone had also told her that walking made labor easier, which was important since someone else had said labor would be the worst pain she would ever experience in her whole life.

That sounded pretty grim to me, but people said stuff like that to Debra all the time. "Get lots of rest—you'll need it for later." "You won't get any sleep for at least the first three months." "Enjoy your freedom now. Your life will never be the same." You had to wonder why people had kids at all, or at least second children.

Even though he was due in mid-February (according to the latest revised ultrasound), everyone at our house but me was becoming more and more excited about this baby. Teal's room already had baby clothes in the drawers, diapers stacked in the changing table, a stroller parked in the closet and a baby swing with a stuffed bear sitting in it.

Only I wanted time to stop. But of course it didn't.

At our last breakfast together with Beauty, Debra mentioned again that her doctor was worried about her blood pressure being a little high. I couldn't process half of what she said, because all I could think of was Beauty at that point.

I wanted to spoil Beauty this one last meal together, to give her crunchy bacon and bits of toast dipped in egg, but instead I gave her kibble and counted *one Mississauga, two Mississauga*...same as always. I looked at her sitting too straight and tall, her golden eyes watching me, her dark chocolate ears slightly lifted.

I couldn't believe it. I'd gotten suckered in again.

My heart hammered hard in my throat as I realized I couldn't really separate my feelings about her from the way I felt about the other Beauty. Even though I had tried not to love her, I loved her twice as much. "Go," I finally told her, and then tried to smile as I listened to the happy crunching. I lay down on the floor beside her watering dish to watch one last time as she lapped up her water. Then she moved over my face to lap me up.

Mom slammed a cupboard and Beauty startled a bit. "Easy. It's OK." I stroked across her head gently, gently. When I stopped she nudged me for more. "No, let's go out for a walk." Beauty wagged her agreement enthusiastically.

But Deb didn't want to come this time. She said she didn't feel very well, although I thought she might just be giving me time alone with Beauty.

Snapped into her leash a few minutes later, Beauty trotted ahead of me, as happy as if it were her birthday. With every step her tail wagged hellos to the world. Hello to the cat hunkered down underneath the neighbor's car. Hello to the crow cawing at us from the edge of the convenience-store garbage can. Hello to Marnie, my favorite baby-sitting customer, as her mom took her to kindergarten. Hello to Scott as he headed toward school.

"Hey, Beauty, I'm gonna miss you, girl." Scott bent down and patted Beauty's head. Just the way his hand moved over her so gently made tears blur everything in front of me. "You're tough, Elizabeth," he continued, and shook his head. "I don't know how you can do it."

Finally, I could feel one tear sliding down my face.

Scott looked up at me. "Oh geez. I'm sorry."

"I don't get why people think I can do this so easily. I hate that. And you think I'm tough? I'm not. I just don't have a choice. I never have a choice about anything." I yanked Beauty's leash and began to run with her.

"Elizabeth! Elizabeth!" Scott called as he chased after me. Finally he caught my coat and pulled me toward him. "Elizabeth," he said as he hugged me. Then he found my face, held my chin for a moment and kissed me. I didn't remember to loosen my lips but his mouth felt so soft I felt my own mouth soften. My lips somehow parted and I felt his lips open. Now what? I wondered, somewhere in my head. Now nothing. Beauty whimpered and we finally broke apart. "Call me, just to talk, later," Scott said. "You know I'll always be here for you."

Oh, sure! Scott was never there for me—let's face it. He spent all his time with Gwen. And with his kiss still on my lips, I heard his last line as a goodbye, which made everything worse. But Beauty just trotted away, still waving hello. That's the trouble with dogs, they don't ever wave good-bye.

After she'd done her business, we swung round for home. At the house, her whole body wagged when I slid the van door open. Big noise or not, there was nothing like a car ride to get her all excited. She climbed in and pushed her nose through the partly opened back window. I sat in the back with her, my arm draped around her shoulders, giving Mom the chauffeur's domain of the entire front seat.

We drove away, past sights we'd seen together a thousand times, past the hill where I Rollerbladed and fell down, with her scrambling after to rescue me. Would she remember any of this? Would she remember me? I almost wished she wouldn't, so she couldn't feel this pain that I felt.

As we rolled into the Lions Foundation parking lot, we saw trainers walking dogs in the back. I'd always felt a thrill to see them, only not now. "That will be you tomorrow," I whispered when Beauty raised her ears to study them.

Inside the building, a huge black Lab greeted us, slowly, calmly. "Hello, Silver," I said. Silver was a retired guide dog who'd been adopted by one of the trainers. He was often left free to wander the building. He sat back down near the top of the stairs, ready to welcome someone else.

Mom and I headed for the coordinator's office. She showed us into the room and got us to sit down on the wooden armchairs. By now my eyes burned and I couldn't talk, not even to answer her small talk about the weather or how Beauty was doing.

"OK, so I'll leave you two alone for a few minutes," she finally said, and opened the door to leave.

Mom actually kissed Beauty's muzzle and held my shoulder for a moment. "I'm sorry, Elizabeth."

Then the door closed behind her and I tried so hard not to cry. Which always makes things worse—same as if you try not to laugh. Beauty licked at me and started to get silly, as if to cheer me up. She dashed around the office, bending down on her front legs, inviting me to play.

"You don't understand. I have to say good-bye."

I finally dove at her and caught her in a cross between a headlock and a hug. "I'll always love you, Beauty. Just remember that."

And the door opened again. The coordinator snapped on the leash and Beauty trotted away, still wagging her tail.

"Come on, let's hurry," Mom said. She was afraid we'd hear the moment when Beauty was locked in the kennel—her howls of realization as the gate shut—the same way we had with Beauty I. But the building had been renovated, and the kennel was too far away.

Mom threw her arm around me as if to hold me up and we walked together that way, back to the car. After she climbed into the driver's seat, Mom pulled out a handkerchief and blew her nose.

Mom was crying? That made me feel better, for some reason, and I reached over to hug her. But as we clung to each other, crying and hugging, the sound of her cell phone interrupted us.

"Hello? What! But it's too early!" Mom paused and I saw her whole face crinkle as she squeezed her eyes shut tight. "No, Debra. You're both going to be all right. Stay calm. We're on our way."

Kyle

January

As misguided as it sounds, maybe getting hit by that car was a lucky thing. It got me Maddie back, and I went to the teen support group as I'd promised Shawna. I even spoke to them about retinopathy and how important good blood-sugar control could be to avoid that kind of complication. Ryan thought my new "do-gooder" thing was just another successful chick-attracting scheme, since Maddie never seemed to leave my side now. But trying to help others actually made me feel better about myself. Less helpless.

I also ended up at the eye specialist again and when I complained about my shrinking eyes and wearing sunglasses all the time, he suggested special Mylar eye covers. I had to bring him pictures of me with my former, normal eyes and have molds taken, but afterwards, I wore two contact-lens-type covers.

"I love them," Maddie told me. "They look just like your old eyes. Except…"

"Except what?"

"Well, your new eyes always seem to look up. You look hopeful, or optimistic."

"I feel hopeful," I realized, grinning.

"Really? What happened? Tell me! Did you manage to convince someone at one of those schools?"

"I'm not exactly sure. Of the four that Shawna had

numbers for, I got hold of one trainer from Canine Vision in Oakville. Her name is January and she's coming to interview me next week."

Maddie chuckled. "January is coming in January. I think that's a lucky sign."

"Me too." Whatever Amber or Jack or any of my other references had written or told Canine Vision obviously hadn't turned them off me.

The thing was I wanted to be enthusiastic. I wanted to believe a dog would be the solution to my problem. But even if the animals were terrific, could I control my fear enough to trust and look after one?

Mom acted as though if she only cleaned up the house well enough, everything would be fine; I'd get over my fear and be accepted into the program immediately. She had the carpets and upholstery steam-cleaned, reorganized the kitchen cupboards, and hollered at Shawna and Dad to put away their shoes, backpack, briefcase, whatever. "If we have clutter everywhere, they'll think the house isn't safe for a guide dog."

I didn't really get that one, but cleaning's Mom's approach to anyone visiting. It was a rainy, cold day when January arrived, and the moment she stepped into the house I smelled a kind of wet-wool smell.

Shawna poked me. "She's brought a dog!"

"What kind?" I asked. "Say it's not a German shepherd, *please*."

"It's not. It's tall and black with curly hair. Soooo

cute. Promise you won't screw up, Kyle, promise! Here, take these dog treats. They were free samples in the mail that I saved just in case."

I tucked the bone-shaped cookies into my pockets.

"At least this way the dog's going to like you," she said. "Shh, shh, she's coming. Stand up. Smile!" she poked me again. "Let's meet her halfway in the hall."

I went where Shawna dragged me.

"Hello, you must be Kyle," a breezy voice said. "I'm January McDonald from Canine Vision."

"Hi," I said extending my hand. January shook it.

"And down to my right is King. King, this is Kyle." Could I do this—reach out in the darkness to pat some dog named King? It was like being a kid in the dark again, with no night-light. What was out there? Would the animal snap off my fingers? Instead I held out a dog bone and felt a small tug as the dog took it. Then I stretched my hand farther out and touched fuzzy hair. "Um, what kind of dog is he?" I asked, resisting the urge to snap back my hand.

"A standard poodle. Mostly we have Labs, but King is a good dog for allergies."

"I'm not allergic," I said quickly.

"That's good. Don't worry, we have all that information on record. Now, where can we get better acquainted?"

"Sorry—this way. Just follow me." I led her into the living room, which is kind of a misnomer, because

nobody even breathes, never mind lives, in there. Mom
and Dad kept the best, newest furniture in there. We had
green leather couches and a beige rug. The coffee table
was a deep mahogany wood one that Mom had inherited
from an aunt.

I sat on the easy chair to give January more room on
the couch.

"Sit, King. Good boy," she said. Then she
explained what would happen if I was chosen for the
program. I'd have to spend one month at the Canine
Vision facility, with almost no outside visits or activities,
except for the odd Sunday.

"But what about regular school?" I broke in. It was
hard staying on top of all the reading without being away
for so long. I couldn't imagine being away from home—
the place where I mostly knew where everything was;
where everyone looked after me and didn't expect me to
cope for myself.

"Oh, the session you'd be attending would be over
the summer."

She continued her explanation. The first few days
I'd have to orient myself to the school, find my way
around, get used to my room. Then I'd try out different dogs and learn to harness and groom the animals,
as well as the basic commands. By the end of the week,
I'd have my own dog. I'd be left to bond with it for a
whole afternoon.

I hoped my face didn't show the fear that clawed at

my insides. How could any dog bond with a person afraid of it?

Next we'd train together through indoor obstacle courses, and then we'd work on the outdoors. They would take us to Hamilton and Toronto and with our dogs, we'd go on buses and subways.

No, no, it couldn't be possible.

The last exercise January told me about was where they dropped you off with your dog somewhere in Oakville, and then you'd be expected to make your way back to the Lions Foundation building.

"But how can you?" I asked.

"You'll have trained in a lot of the spots before then, and you're expected to ask for directions."

I bit down on my lip to resist saying how impossible the whole process sounded.

"Would you like to go outside and try King now?" January asked.

"Sure, sure. Yeah. That would be good." I nodded enthusiastically so my fear wouldn't show. *This dog won't bite*, I told myself as I practiced deep breathing. We stepped outside.

Luckily, I didn't feel like a complete loser in our own neighborhood. The weeks of going to school by myself had paid off.

"Take the harness," January told me.

I grabbed hold of a stiff leather handle.

"Now what?" I asked.

"Give King the command to go forward."

I hesitated. "Go forward," I said stiffly and then felt a tug. I followed behind, feeling happy to walk quickly without waving a white cane in front of me. Suddenly the pulling stopped. "Hey, we're not at the curb yet. I know this block. What's wrong with the dog?"

"Tell him 'Forward' again."

"Forward," I told him. Nothing happened. "Forward!" I snapped. *Stupid dog, how could he possibly show me up like this? You rely on the stupid animal and then he won't do what he's told.*

"Reach your hand up, Kyle," January told me.

I lifted my arm and my hand banged into a hanging branch. Since the last time I had walked this way, the wind or a storm must have snapped it. "Oh, geez. Did the dog understand that I might hit myself against that branch?"

"Yes, he did," January answered.

Had I just flunked the interview? "Good dog, Good King." I fumbled in my pocket for another one of the bones that Shawna had slipped me. Then I held it out. I wanted just to be grateful to the animal. He had saved me a scratch or a bump at the least. Still, I could feel my hand shaking. *Don't bite me. Don't slobber*, I willed silently instead. King took the cookie and I heard him crunching. I pulled back my hand. Phew.

"Did you see the segment on the Discovery Channel about the guide dog that saved its owner from live wires downed by a storm?"

"No." I couldn't help smiling and shaking my head.

"What's wrong?" January asked.

"Nothing, nothing. It just seems that everyone in the world watched that program except me."

"Do you have any questions about the program, Kyle?"

"Um, no...yes. Does anyone ever flunk?"

"Not exactly. If we've accepted someone into the program, that person would never flunk. But sometimes we find we can't match up the right dog with the right person."

Right dog, right person. Hmm. What dog could possibly be the right one for me?

CHAPTER 13

Elizabeth Alone

Mom may have told Deb to stay calm but I could tell Mom wasn't going to. She threw me the cell phone to call Dad while she booted it all the way home. "Nothing to worry about," she lied as Debra climbed in the van. "Call the doctor," she called back to me. "Give Liz the number."

"What should I say?" I asked as the phone rang.

Deb just grabbed the cell phone from me. "Yes, yes. It's Deb Kerr." Pause. Debra moaned and spoke low. "I feel awful. My head hurts. My back aches." She moaned again. "No, but my membranes ruptured." Pause. "We're almost there." Debra moaned again and leaned her head against the window. She closed her eyes and slumped.

"Mom, Mom!" I cried. "Deb's passed out."

Mom glanced over from the steering wheel. I heard her suck in a breath. "It's going to be fine," she hissed at me. "We're here now." She veered around toward the emergency entrance. "Run in and grab someone," she told me.

I ran to the door, pushing my hip against the handle to bump it open. Then I tore over to the desk. "Help me, please! Something's wrong with my sister and she's going to have a baby."

"Where is she?" the lady behind the desk asked.

I threw out my arm to point back at the car. "Outside."

"Hank, can you help? This girl's sister is in trouble."

"She's in that van." I pointed it out as he grabbed a wheelchair and headed toward it. He yanked open the door where Deb sat leaning against Mom, still out and pale as snow. The man lifted Deb, who flopped like a rag doll in the chair.

Then he rolled her into the hospital, with Mom and I on his tail.

"Can you fill out these forms?" the lady at the desk called.

Mom stopped for a second, pivoting as though faking a basketball pass.

"It's OK. I can do it," I offered, and she continued after Deb and the guy named Hank.

Forms are always a pain. *Last name first, first name last, birth date*— would it be month, day, year or day, month, year? *Address, mailing address if different*. What was our postal code? The numbers disappeared from my head.

Name of doctor, reason for stay. I rushed through the questions as fast as I could but it took forever and I had to cross out a bunch of answers when I put them in the wrong spot.

I gave the desk lady the clipboard and form back but she

was talking on the phone. Then she picked it up and looked it over.

"Please, could you tell me where they would have gone?" I asked desperately.

"Fourth floor, maternity."

I dashed to the elevator, which I shared with a woman carrying a silver balloon. "Welcome Baby," the words across the inflated heart read. The elevator lurched to a stop as the number four lit up. *Sish*. I pushed out frantically, not even knowing which way to go. When Balloon Lady squeezed by, I decided to follow her.

She asked at the nurse's station about her daughter, who was having a baby, and the nurse pointed her to the waiting room. "I'll tell your son-in-law you're here."

I asked about Deb and the nurse made me head for the waiting room too.

"Mom, is she OK?" I asked when I saw my mother's face buried in her hands. She looked up and I saw tears streaked down the sides of her face. "Oh, my god, what's wrong?"

"She's having convulsions. They're going to have to do an emergency Caesarean."

"What does that mean?" I asked, but she buried her head back into her hands. "Mom? Mom!" How could it all have turned so bad so quickly?

When Dad finally arrived, I heard the whole explanation, although I processed only bits.

"Preeclampsia," Mom called it. Deb's blood pressure

had shot up too high and she could go into a coma. The baby might make it if they get him out in time; that was, if his lungs were mature.

"What about Deb?" I asked. "She'll be OK for sure, won't she?"

Mom turned and looked at me but she didn't say a word.

I ran out of the room. *I can't lose my sister*, I thought. I don't want to lose the baby, either, but Deb—it couldn't be possible. It wouldn't happen, and yet I could see the way she had slumped against the van window. She had looked…dead already. I paced back and forth in the halls. The lady with the balloon was going to see her new grandson now. Oh, sure, she got a healthy daughter and baby. How fair was that?

I kept pacing. I couldn't stop. Then I heard a voice.

"Little sister?"

"Rolph!" I snarled. Then I turned, rushed at him and started punching his chest. He didn't stop me for a minute, but then grabbed both my fists, lifted them and dropped them over his shoulders as he hugged me. He was crying too.

"I've been in town for two days and when your father called me, I couldn't believe it. It's so early."

"Elizabeth!" I heard my mother's voice. "The baby's out. Come see him."

Rolph and I rushed to Mom and we followed a nurse into a room full of glass incubators. There I met my nephew, too impossibly tiny, waving angry fists around. On his head, he wore a tiny blue woolen tuque. His eyes were covered in a blindfold.

"He's not…" I couldn't finish.

"No, they have to put him under special lights, so they cover his eyes to protect them."

I sighed. "Debra?" I asked Mom.

"We'll know soon."

* * *

I felt so awful that night—like everything good had been sucked out of the world. My chest and stomach ached and my eyes burned. If Beauty had been here I would have walked her, and some of my tightness would have unwound. But of course she wasn't. So I slipped downstairs in my pajamas and sat by her crate for a while. How was she doing in the kennel? Had to be better than I was. I sighed.

Then I got my pillow and blanket and bunked half in and half out of Beauty's crate. With my head inside, I could smell dog and feel dog and almost see dog. It made me calmer. There I could sleep.

The next morning I woke up aching a little less. You can only feel so awful for so long. Mom and Dad were already getting ready to go to the hospital. When the phone rang, Mom jumped to answer it. "It's for you."

Scott, I thought. *He does care.*

"Hi, Liz. Are you OK?" Alicia asked. "I mean, I know how rough it must be for you to give up Beauty."

I sighed, and then filled her in on just how much worse things had gotten since giving up my dog.

"Wow." She sucked in a long breath and stayed quiet for a moment. Then she spoke again. "You know Debra can't die, don't you?" Another quiet moment. I just couldn't answer. Alicia continued quickly. "Sure, she may be really sick now, but she's the in best hospital around. Honest, Liz, I wouldn't just say it. My cousin's a nurse there."

"But you had to see her. She looked so bad. And Teal. He's tiny, with tubes stuck all over him. He wears this little blindfold, and he waves his arms like he's angry at the world already."

"Poor little guy. But you know what? I have a good feeling about all this. They'll come home soon."

Home. "I didn't tell you—Rolph came to the hospital."

"Oh." She paused for a moment. "Well, most people who have babies live with their partners. You can't stop that. Is he moving back near here or staying in L.A.?"

"I don't know." It was too depressing to think about, but I realized there was a bargain I should be making in my mind, in order to keep Debra and Teal alive. A bargain I wasn't ready to make. "I gotta go now. We're leaving for the hospital."

"OK. Call me when things turn around."

"Sure," I said. "Bye." I slipped the receiver back into the cradle. Then quickly, I snatched it up again and keyed in Scott's number. He'd told me to call, after all.

His dad picked up. "Gwen, hi. He left for your place

twenty minutes ago. Should be there soon."

He thought I was Gwen. I didn't feel like correcting him. "Um, um, OK. Thanks." I hung up. *You know I'll always be here for you.* That's what Scott had told me. I thought about Beauty then—her golden eyes, the way they looked straight into mine; her big, heavy paws. She would have always been there for me if I hadn't given her back to Canine Vision.

"Let's go," Dad called. "You coming, Liz?"

I nodded and followed him out to the van.

Ordinary things continue to happen in the world, even as awful things happen in your own family. As we drove to the hospital, I saw cars turning into the mall parking lot. A bus stopped and some kids from my school got off. Farther on, I saw a lady pushing a baby in the carriage—healthy baby, healthy mom. An ordinary thing. An ordinary thing everyone expects.

Then we drove behind an ambulance, the light flashing, the siren wailing. Not a normal thing. We weren't the only family in the world something bad was happening to. We turned in after the ambulance into the visitors' parking lot and headed into the hospital up to intensive care. Mom and Dad went in to see Debra first, and I stood waiting in the hall. I could hear machines *sishing* and *beeping*. Someone talked quietly about something serious; someone else answered over and over, "Yes, yes, I understand." How could a person understand anything in this place?

I could smell medicine, strong as cleaning detergent. I started to feel bleak, like a gray, rainy day. Then Rolph showed up at my side, a blue teddy bear tucked under his arm and a tray of coffee cups in his hands. I felt angry, like I wanted to hit him all over again.

"Here, I brought you some hot chocolate." Rolph handed me a cup. "Have a cookie to go with it."

My mouth filled with sweetness even though my heart felt like a pointy rock. Rolph's eyes looked bloodshot and glazed. Purple shadowed them. His tone of voice sounded pleading.

I should make the bargain. He's trying so hard. Everyone screws up sometimes, everyone. He drank; he lost Deb and the baby. Now everyone will lose Deb and the baby if I don't do it.

"She's awake and asking for you." Mom poked her head out of the ICU.

Rolph stepped forward hopefully.

"No, for Elizabeth."

I rushed in. My sister smiled at me and I started to cry.

"I'm OK," she whispered to me. "Tell me the truth. How is he?"

I thought for a moment. "Rolph?"

"No, Teal. They tell me he's fine but I don't trust them. I want to hear it from you."

"He's so little, Deb, it's scary. And he's wearing a blindfold. But all that's supposed to be all right."

"Is he breathing on his own?"

I shook my head and Deb turned away. "I was so sure I ate right and exercised well."

I shrugged my shoulders. "You did."

"I must have done something wrong," Deb said.

"No." I swallowed, feeling pretty sure about that. "Things just happen sometimes." I knew now that Deb felt as bleak as I did, but I had to make her feel better. "It doesn't matter anyway. If you get strong again and Teal grows big, we'll all forget this…"

"If Teal grows big…" Deb smiled at me. "Go see him, Elizabeth. Tell him he has to grow big for his mom."

I smiled back at her. The sheet of gray lifted and the edges sticking out of my heart rounded and smoothed. I could believe it all for Deb, and I would do as she asked. "I'll go see him right now."

"Liz?"

"Yeah, Deb."

"Send in Rolph."

"Sure."

I stepped out of the room and told Rolph to go on in. He looked relieved as he walked through the doorway. Dad and Mom came with me as I headed toward the intensive care nursery. I stepped up to the little glass box where Teal lived. Then I made the bargain, blinking back tears. *Debra can go back to Rolph, so long as she and Teal live.*

Out loud I said, "Listen, baby Teal. This is very important. You have to keep growing and gaining weight and getting big. Your mom needs you. And I need you both."

CHAPTER 14

Kyle

Summer

If anyone had told me that I'd be going to school to get a dog—on my summer vacation, no less—I would have thought they were crazy. Still, who could have predicted that I would get diabetes or go blind? And that I would have to conquer my fear of the dark and—hopefully—dogs, to survive? Dogs. Slobbering, growling, snapping...ugh, would I ever be able to do it?

The night before I had to report in at Canine Vision, I tossed around in my bed, pressing the voice button on my alarm clock, listening to time passing and wondering just how I could back out. I felt hot and nauseous by the time the electronic rooster crowed. And I felt even worse later, as I followed along on the building tour. Which may have accounted for my reaction to Angela, the girl walking beside me: pure irritation. January had introduced us all and Angela was a law student at Queen's, Dad's old school. When January showed us the kennels, Angela acted far too eager. "When can we work with the dogs?"

"Tomorrow," January answered.

"We get our dog tomorrow," Angela repeated, all breathy with excitement, and something else. Joy?

I felt jealous. I wanted to be excited and happy instead of sick and tired and afraid.

"No, you'll just work with different animals, heeling them," January answered. "We want to see how you work with them. Come this way, please."

"Careful of that corner," Angela warned me.

I felt the impact of it in my side just as she said it. "Hey, aren't you supposed to be blind?"

"I *am* legally blind. I see light and shadows and in the morning, the outlines of shapes. As the day wears on, my sight gets worse."

Fine for her—at least she could see a little, and she wasn't afraid of dogs. Bet she didn't need to check her blood sugar four times a day, either.

Every wrong turn I made, every time I stumbled, Angela pointed it out and commented on it. "The cafeteria's over here," she told me at suppertime, when I wanted to turn the other way. "I can get us more sugar if you need some for your coffee." How did she even know that's what I was pawing the middle of the table for?

And she practically gurgled about getting a dog. "I love Labs. They're the friendliest animals. Here's the sugar," she said, handing me a jar.

"I'm diabetic. I need sweetener," I told her sharply.

"I'll say. Here." She took the jar back and gave me a couple of small paper sachets. I ripped open the tops and dumped them into my coffee, stirring *clankety-clank* for a long time.

"Maybe you should get the cook to put your coffee in a blender," she suggested.

I sipped at my cup without answering, and then sputtered and choked. "What the heck!" I spat out the coffee. It tasted awful. The sweetener must have gone bad or…

Angela laughed. "Whoops! Must have given you the salt instead."

Still coughing, I wanted to kill her. And then suddenly, I couldn't help chuckling. Salt in my coffee became the funniest thing that had happened to me in a long time, and I laughed so long I had to fight tears. And while I was laughing, I stopped hating Angela.

Later, back in my room, exhausted, I lay back on my bed and heard the most incredibly beautiful voice singing. The words called to me sadly, sweetly. I tried to resist but ended up grabbing my guitar and following the melody with my chords. It was an Irish lullaby and it could have lured sailors to their grave and, certainly, me down the halls. I couldn't stand it anymore. I had to find out who the voice belonged to. I grabbed my cane, followed the sound a few doors down and knocked.

"Hi, Kyle." It was Angela. How could someone so irritating sing like such an angel? "Just so we're clear from the start, I'm engaged."

"Oh, bad luck for me," I said sarcastically. Then I invited her to the lounge, brought my guitar out and played her some of the songs I'd written. She picked up the harmony on Maddie's song.

"Too bad about your girlfriend," she said when we finished. "I broke off with my first fiancé. Well, actually, I just beat him to the punch."

"That's where you're wrong. Maddie and I are solid. You'll meet her on our last Sunday."

"Really? That song sounded so...oh, well. When I went blind, I had to find a whole new set of friends. And my old boyfriend couldn't see *me* anymore, only what I had lost."

"Mmm. Too bad for you." Maddie and I were different too, now. Didn't every relationship go through changes? Still, what Angela said needled me.

And she needled me even more the next day. When we walked outside, I felt really nervous. Fast moving cars tore around out there, backing up, pulling away without warning. And on top of that, I knew that my gait was crooked and that I confused my left with my right.

"Hey, that's the third time you've bumped into me. Sidewalk hog," Angela said to me. Then she nagged at January. "Why can't we work with a dog right away?"

"We want to observe the way you walk. Some of the animals don't work well with people who veer to one side or step unevenly," January explained.

Thanks to Angela, everyone now knew I veered. Maybe no dog could match my gait.

"I just really want a black Lab," she whined. By now everyone in the school had to know that, too.

"Don't be such a breedist," I told her.

"Oh, my gosh, Kyle made a joke. Everyone? Did you hear that?"

Next day, Angela made fun of me when we were working on collars and harnesses and I put the collar on wrong. How could I get it on straight, really, when I expected teeth to sink into my hands at any moment?

"You're gonna strangle your dog." Then, "You sure you wanna give him one of your animals?" she asked a trainer.

I knew she was teasing. The trainer just laughed too. Angela couldn't know she was poking hot fire into a kindling-wood self-esteem. Still, I felt my face burning and wished she'd just go away.

Happily, I couldn't put the harness on wrong, we just had to hold it out and the dog put its head through it. The trainer explained that this was how they gauged the dog's willingness. If the animal didn't eagerly go for the harness, it would have disqualified itself from the program. Later on, we might realize our dogs were sick or ready to be retired if they avoided it. On healthy, average days, the dog would step in happily. Good thing, too, or I might have ended up walking the dog backwards.

Next day, Angela razzed me about whispering my commands: "Sit! Heel! Lie down! Stay!" She laughed herself silly when the dogs I tried didn't listen. And then suddenly I was too annoyed at her to be afraid of the dogs. "Stay," I

barked at one dog. The dog licked my hand for a second
and I cringed, but when I walked away, it stayed.
Involuntarily, I smelled my fingers. No rotten-meat smell.
Good.

I came back to the dog and patted it. The animal—a
chocolate Lab, the trainer told me—didn't smell too bad at
all. It seemed familiar, too, somehow. The dog nudged me.

"Go ahead, pat Beauty some more," the trainer said.

"What did you say her name was? Beauty?" Shaking, I
scratched the top of the dog's head. It couldn't be *her* dog.
They probably named lots of them the same. Didn't I hear
that they assigned each litter one letter of the alphabet?
Buster, Beamer, Baxter, Beauty—they had to use the same
names over and over.

"Beauty? What kind of name is that for a dog? Mind
you, she is as big as a horse, don't you think?" Angela
asked, always showing off the little vision she had left.

I could feel the dog's head leaning into the scratch. I
forced myself not to pull away. If I could get used to living
in darkness without a night-light, couldn't I force myself to
live with a dog?

"Hey, Beauty seems to like you," the trainer said.

My hand stopped shaking as I stroked the dog's back. It
didn't seem all that big, and it acted so docile. And if it was
her dog it had already saved my life once, to hear the girl
from the park tell it. Maybe I could learn to trust this dog.

What had the trainer told me? If they couldn't match us
up with an animal, or if there was some other personality

problem, we'd be sent home early on. That meant that every day I survived put me one day closer to success.

Day four took us down obstacle courses. I tried out Chopin, Fenway, Digby, King and Beauty again. *No more shaking*, I told myself. *This has to work*. But even with my talking watch to help keep my left and rights straight, I made lots of mistakes. And I had to force myself not to curse. I didn't want them to send me home because of a personality problem, after all.

On Thursday we were supposed to be assigned our dogs. We all had to return to our rooms and wait. I wanted the dog that acted so gentle—the one that listened to me and didn't smell. But who was I kidding? I would have been happy with any animal. Just so long as the trainer didn't come to tell me to pack my things and go home.

The knock at the door came, and I forced myself to slowly walk over and open it.

"Kyle, this is your guide dog. Beauty, this is Kyle, your new owner."

"Yeah!" I couldn't help cheering. I bent down to the dog and she licked my face all over. I pulled away just a little, but continued patting her and then slung one arm around her.

"I take it you like our decision."

"Oh, yeah. Geez, thanks. I love this dog." I listened to myself as I stroked Beauty. I did sound sincere. Well, I didn't hate her, anyway.

"I'll leave you two to get acquainted." The door shut again and I just sat there, my arm still draped over Beauty.

"Look, I'm sorry. I have no idea what to do with you, what dogs like, anything. I don't know my left from my right. I veer when I walk…"

My heart stopped when I felt a heavy paw land on one of my shoulders. It was the weirdest thing. Like the dog was trying to reassure me and tell me, "Hey, that's OK, don't worry about it."

The paw felt like an anchor and it weighed me down, but it felt OK, not scary at all. I felt rooted, and in that instant, I felt loved. Who would have imagined an animal could do that for me?

Elizabeth

July

It took a whole month for Teal to come home, and five months later—despite my bargain about them going to live with Rolph if they survived—Teal and Debra were still at home with us. Rolph came around a lot and that made me nervous, but he always behaved like the perfect gentleman, considerate and generous.

So it didn't surprise me that on the day Debra got her new picture book, *Camel on a Surfboard*, in the mail and Teal blew his first raspberry, Rolph decided to celebrate by buying Teal a jogging stroller. Also in the mail with Deb's advance copies came the invitation to Beauty's graduation.

When Deb felt too wrecked from another sleepless night to even try the stroller out, I volunteered. I called Scott, too. With Gwen away at camp, I knew he had the time; and I wanted to sort out my feelings about Beauty.

I'd immediately told Mom I wouldn't go to guide-dog grad—what was the point? We weren't going to foster any more puppies; not with Teal around.

"Well, you do all the work, Elizabeth," Mom said. "So that's entirely up to you. As far as a puppy and Teal are concerned, it would be good for both to get used to each other. I mean, blind people do have babies."

I shrugged my shoulders and grabbed my Rollerblades from the cupboard. Well, I wasn't going to jog with that stroller, and I'd seen other people blade with their baby buggies. Scott met me at the park with his skates. "I can tell Mom thinks I should go," I explained to him as I strapped mine on.

"Of course. You get to see Beauty doing the job you raised her for. You meet her new owner. Gee, I wanna go. When is it?"

I told him the date and time as we skated around the park, Teal gurgling and perfecting his raspberry technique. But I also said I still wasn't sure. If I went, I knew I'd be suckered into training another puppy for Canine Vision.

Then we headed up the hill. Hard work on the shins, as I dug in the sides of the wheels to climb.

Just like the last time, I considered taking my skates

off but found I couldn't. "Watch Teal a moment. I'm going down," I said to Scott. Then I pushed myself off. I didn't hunker down, not even in the beginning. I held out my arms in a V toward the sky. The wind pulled at my hair and I yelled all the way down. I started to straighten my knees a little. When I saw the grate, I imagined throwing myself on the ground again but then thought, *Nah, I'll take the grate head on*. I bent my knees. Down, down...faster and faster...

Then I straightened, jumped up and over, and landed. Perfect balance. I straightened totally till I stood tall: queen of the universe, master of destiny. I raised my arms and hands. "Woo-hoo!" I hollered. I continued rolling on gravity alone.

Then, for no real good reason, I pitched forward and fell. *Ow!*

"You all right?" Scott asked.

"Peachy," I answered, dusting off my knees. Suddenly, memories from the last wipeout with Beauty came back to me—how she'd galloped after me, looked for help from that stranger and then allowed me to climb up, using her back as a crutch; lapping at my scrapes even as I hollered at her. She was going to make such a good guide dog, and I missed her so badly.

I took a deep breath, blinking back tears. Then I headed back up the hill to take over Teal so Scott could try. "OK, so you're right. Let's go to Beauty's grad," I told him at the top.

We took turns down the hill and I never wiped out
again. As we headed home, we chatted about life in gen-
eral, just like old times. "So Rolph bought the stroller—
neat, huh? Does he live with you guys now?"

"No," I answered carefully as I pushed the stroller
forward. I didn't want to explain about how Debra needed to keep space between them in case Alcoholics
Anonymous didn't work out. "Rolph just wants to spend
time with Teal."

"So he's not working in L.A. anymore?" Scott
asked, as though that were the most incredible thing in
the world.

"Some things are more important, I guess." I
walked more quickly because Teal was starting to fuss.
"Wouldn't you give up a job to stay close to your family?"

"My family—meaning you? When we're thirty? I
hope we'll both travel around the world. Together, of
course. Not stick around here."

Teal's gurgling turned into nattering and Scott
looked edgy. "Is he going to scream all the way home?"

I shook my head and sped up even more, which
worked. Teal's head began to sag and his entire upper
body leaned to the side of the stroller. Within a couple
of minutes he was asleep like a dead weight. I tucked his
unconscious body back straight in the stroller and we
continued walking and talking about all kinds of other
stuff. I told Scott about my mom's poetry suite winning
an honorable mention in the CBC contest. "She's going

to read it on the radio and—you're gonna love this, she's been shopping for the perfect outfit."

"Your mom, worried about what to wear on radio?" We both chuckled.

"She's in such a good mood. She let Dad buy a new notebook computer."

"He must be in heaven."

"Nah, he works on the train now, instead of napping. Dad's always doing staff evaluations. Regal Trust had another re-org and gave him even more people."

"Still, the notebook should have done the trick." Scott shrugged. "Whenever my dad hates his job, he buys himself a toy. You should see the cool remote-control airplane he has. It looks so real when it's up in the air."

"Your mom's OK with that?'

"Yeah. When she's unhappy it's kitchen gadgets. Have you ever tried an apple-peeling machine? The whole peel comes off in one piece."

Remote-control airplanes, one-piece apple peelers and all kinds of other stupid things, that's what we talked about on the trip home. Apart from Scott being a little impatient with Teal, I knew he was the boy I wanted to be with right now, not when I turned thirty.

As we headed down our block, we saw Dad walking toward the house from the other side—his steps quick and long, as though he were rushing for yet another commuter train.

Then he saw us and slowed down, a big grin creeping across his face.

"He doesn't seem that unhappy to me," Scott said as we both waved.

And Scott was right. Dad's whole face brightened like a birthday cake whenever he looked down at Teal. "Well, work's not everything, as I said. He seems to get a big kick out of the baby."

"Go figure," Scott said, shaking his head. Then he made a little finger gun that he pointed and shot at me. "See you Thursday. My house, six-thirty, right?"

"Right," I answered, smiling. It felt really good to know we were going to Beauty's graduation together. Who else realized how important or how difficult this would be? Only Scott. It was like Rollerblading down that hill and jumping over the grate. I felt triumphant, felt like holding my arms open in a giant V. Scott understood me. Scott was going to be there for me!

CHAPTER 15

Kyle and Beauty

Well, Angela didn't get the dog of her dreams. Instead of a black Lab, she received a golden retriever, Butterscotch. And from that Thursday on, golden retrievers became the absolute best dogs to have, ever, they were so beautiful.

"Who cares what they look like anyway when you can't see, right, Beauty?" I patted my dog, trying to picture the glossiness of her fur rather than the sharpness of her fangs. We sat in the recreation room together with Angela and Butterscotch—me, as usual, strumming my guitar; Angela singing. The others joined in and we started singing an old Elvis tune, "Hound Dog," in honor of our training partners. Everyone really went crazy and when we finished, even the trainers whooped and applauded.

"That was great, Beauty," January said—which was odd, since the dog wasn't howling along or anything. "Kyle, do you know where your dog is?"

Panicking, I felt around on the floor near me to realize

Beauty had gone.

"I paired you with her because I thought you could be strict with her. You should keep the leash tucked under your feet at all times," January said. "Beauty has some strange habits. If I didn't know better, I'd say she just performed an Elvis imitation."

When January handed me back the leash, I forced sternness into my voice. "Beauty, lie down." But relief washed over me when I felt Beauty's back against my legs, and I patted her head ever so gently. "You can't leave me, girl." *Even if someone else could love you better.*

Next morning we were supposed to head to downtown Toronto with our dogs and Angela seemed just as nervous as me. *I'm OK. I'm not scared*, I kept telling myself, just as I had when my bandages had come off my eyes. The results weren't too good that time, either, I reminded myself when we climbed onto our bus and Beauty acted restless.

"Don't get soft on me," January hissed. "Give her a correction!"

I should have done that on my own. I shouldn't have had to be told. Did I think Beauty might still turn on me? Would this be a strike against me? Or was it possible that Beauty herself could flunk these tests? I pulled down hard on the leash so she would lie down and stay put. Then, after a few minutes, I reached down and stroked her. She was up. I tugged the leash again. None of the other dogs were having trouble; *that* I knew.

Angela was telling Butterscotch how perfect she was, as

usual. Really, that dog was a saint.

I started singing under my breath to keep my hands from shaking. "'Our bus driver's gonna buy us all a beer…'" I patted Beauty again. She sank down now. I felt her back again when I got to the third chorus, and she was still down and calm.

A couple of times in Toronto, Beauty seemed to startle at sudden noises—or was that in reaction to me? Could she feel my fear? I hated all the cars and noise. They seemed to be coming from every direction. "Hop up, Beauty," I said at the curb of a noisy intersection. Beauty stepped right to the edge of the sidewalk now. I listened for a break in traffic but none ever came. Luckily, the light actually chirped a signal that it was safe to walk.

Phew. No huge, scary decision for me. "Forward, Beauty," I told her. Back up on the sidewalk, we kept walking and then suddenly Beauty stopped.

"Forward, girl," I said, irritated. This was the middle of the block. I knew Angela and Saint Butterscotch were tail-gating us, ready to make us look stupid. "Did you hear me? I said *Forward*." The bus was one thing; starting at all those noises was another. Now here, for no reason, this stupid dog wasn't going to listen to me. She was going to ruin everything for the both of us. Didn't she understand how important it was that she obeyed? I pulled hard at her leash.

"Kyle, stop!" January yelled to me. "There's a car back-ing up in front of you, just to your left."

As I stood there shaking, I could feel the hot exhaust

blow across my legs. My knees felt all wobbly and I shivered all over.

"Oh geez, she saved me."

"It's what she's trained to do. You just have to pay attention to her when she stops," January told me.

"Good girl, Beauty. Good girl," I repeated as I patted her. I wanted to weep with joy and relief, to throw myself down in gratitude to this dog.

The last Sunday, Maddie came to visit and I told her all that had happened.

"Why do they make you walk around in such a dangerous area? I mean, Toronto's such a busy city."

"But that's the point. It's to prove you can go anywhere you want—do everything."

"Hmmph. A little unrealistic, don't you think?"

At that point I thought of Angela and what she'd said about her ex. It was true. *They only see what you've lost, not what you can do.* I shook my head. I reached to her and kissed her on the cheek.

"What's that for?" she asked.

"Maddie, both you and I know that it's over."

"What, Kyle? What are you saying?"

"Us—I mean, going out together. You still can't handle all this." I waved my hand toward my eyes. "I forced you into it."

Unhappily, she didn't say one word, couldn't think of any way to even try to deny it.

I reached for her and stroked her cheek, which felt wet.

"Aw, Maddie, don't be sad. You've been such a good friend to me. I couldn't have done it without you."

"I can't believe you replaced me with a dog." She half laughed, half choked. "OK, I'm going to walk away now and not cry and make a big scene."

"OK," I said softly.

"Bye, Kyle," I heard from a distance, and I gave a single wave good-bye.

That night I buried myself in music to forget. Angela helped me write a new song for Beauty, although she insisted Butterscotch be in it. In the end, I included the whole guide-dog class.

"So, do you think we'll do OK on the test run?" I asked Angela before we went back to our rooms. For the final exercise tomorrow, the Canine Vision van would drop us off in the middle of Oakville with our dogs, but no instructions, and we'd have to find our way back to the building.

"Well, Butterscotch and I have it in the bag. You and Beauty, I'm afraid, may need extra help." I knew her teasing was a vote of confidence. Still, between Beauty's fears and habits and my own, I didn't know if we deserved it.

* * *

I had to stop at least eight different people to give us directions back to the Lions Foundation building. Left or right, after the fourth block or on block four—who could ever get it straight? I didn't even know who was making the mistakes, the people giving directions or me. And to make matters worse, I thought I could hear the van following at a crawl behind us. The trainers must have thought I was some directionless dweeb. But that was OK with me, as long as I could keep Beauty.

When we crossed what I thought was the last street, I finally stopped on the corner and cheated. "Home, Beauty. Just take us home, girl." I knew that the trainers had walked the dogs all over Oakville and that as long as I was within a reasonable distance of the building, Beauty would find her way. And I was right.

Beauty and I had passed the final test. As far as I was concerned, she'd surpassed all my expectations on our Toronto outing. She was my dog.

That evening, Angela and I practiced and played the song we wrote.

CHAPTER 16

Elizabeth

Graduation I

I should have known I was in trouble since Scott never called me back, over the next week, to confirm. When grad night came, I stood on his steps, waiting. Every hopeful feeling sank lower and lower with the flash of the numbers on my watch. Six-thirty, six forty-five, seven.

Dad hollered from the van window. "We'll have to leave now, Liz. Or we won't make it in time."

By then my heart was pounding from my feet, slow and painful. Scott and I were finished. I turned to leave. Of course, that's when Scott rolled up in a strange car. He was sitting in the back with Gwen, who had returned from camp, obviously. He jumped out and the car backed up and drove away.

"Oh, man, sorry, Liz. Was tonight the night? I went to the beach and forgot."

"Uh-huh." I frowned. Then I threw a wild arrow at Scott, just to see his reaction. "What if it's Gwen?"

"What? Sorry? I don't follow you, Liz. Shouldn't we be going?"

"No, this is important. Maybe if you don't find anyone better by the time you're thirty, maybe Gwen's the one you should marry."

Scott's face suddenly blanched white. Direct hit, I thought, and launched another arrow. "You told her the same thing, didn't you?" He stared down at his feet. "Wow. You're going to keep a big list of girls, just in case you have no one to marry, aren't you?"

Funny thing about that arrow—it hit me, too, right in the chest. It was hard to breathe for a moment. "You know what? I don't want to get married that badly. I'll stay single if I can't find someone better." I headed for the van.

"Elizabeth?" Scott called.

"Forget it, Scott. I have someplace important to be."

We were extra late now, so Dad booted it all the way to the Lions Foundation Building, dropping me off at the door while he parked. As I ran to the lounge area I felt nightmare nervous, like everything would continue to go wrong—the ceremony might be over, or Beauty wouldn't be there or wouldn't know me.

Already the walls of the room were lined with clusters of people and dogs. In the middle, where rows of metal chairs faced attentively forward, a few people already sat, some with dogs at their feet.

Some of the dogs in the middle were puppies, too young to be graduates. One or two actually wore the heavy

black leather Canine Vision collar—dogs at work, waiting to
graduate.

I walked along the walls, checking out all the dogs, looking for Beauty. In an orange coat, the ugliest rat dog ever
jumped all over a young boy. It was small, with a pointy
nose and ears, too much hair around its neck and a skinny,
long tail. The boy actually threw himself down on the floor
with the rat, jumping all over him with the same overenthu-
siastic zeal.

Hearing ear dog, definitely, I told myself. Then I saw
three huge Labs standing together. I quickly scanned for
Beauty. Nope, all black Labs. Next stood a golden retriever
and next to that—my heart started beating harder now—was
a chocolate Lab. Was it her? I squinted, but before I could
be sure, Beauty started barking for me.

Kyle

Graduation I

Graduation night came. A whole twenty-seven days away
from home come to an end. In a way, I couldn't wait to
go back.

I showered and dressed in one-bead colors, beige
pants and a light shirt. A new outfit for a new me; I'd
brought it just in case. Then I brushed Beauty and we
both joined Butterscotch and Angela in the lounge.
Shawna came over to meet "my new girlfriend," as she

called Angela, and Dad and Mom followed.

"Well done, Kyle," Dad said, grabbing and hugging me. "I've always known you possessed great courage. But today you're really making me proud."

Mom hugged me too, and then they went to find themselves some good seats near the front.

"Neither my family nor Butterscotch's foster family can make it," Angela said. Angela hailed all the way from Nova Scotia. "Too bad they couldn't see her in action."

"I only wish Beauty's couldn't come." I stood there, shifting from foot to foot, listening to all the other dogs greeting their former owners. I didn't think I could take it if Beauty wanted to go back to her other family.

Angela kept prattling at me. "So you've got my e-mail address and you're going to write. If we both give up on law school, we could form a group." Yadda yadda yadda. Still no foster family.

Beauty and I waited so long, I started to feel annoyed on her behalf. It was one thing to have a time conflict, but quite another just to stand her up.

And then suddenly, Beauty started barking. And I could hear it in her tone. It was a cross between yelping with pain and howling for joy. She'd found her previous owner. Listening to her, I thought my heart would crack in pieces. She loved that other person; I knew she did. And I wanted Beauty happy. She pulled forward and I heard a young girl's voice. Oh geez, it was the girl who'd found me in the street, Elizabeth. So Beauty wasn't just a

Lab from a different B litter. For a moment I hated the girl. She had sight, and Beauty's love.

"Could you just wait till I take off her harness?" What an idiot thing to say to someone who's given up her dog for you. And the one thing I can never do is backtrack or apologize. I just got nastier and nastier.

Which made Elizabeth finally recognize me. "You're the liar who accused Beauty of biting you."

I wanted to explain to her about my horrific experience with Max the German shepherd, and how I'd hallucinated about it the night she and Beauty saved me. I opened my mouth but hesitated as, in my head, I heard this girl's laughter in the park.

Then the head trainer called the graduating class to the front of the room, and the ceremony began.

CHAPTER 17

Elizabeth

Graduation II

I rushed toward her, and her barking sounded almost like a howl. She didn't just sound happy to see me, she sounded desperate. I reached out to her and she leapt up to me.

"Could you just wait till I take off her harness?" a familiar-sounding voice said. "She's supposed to be working, after all." I looked past Beauty to see her new owner. He was young and tall, with black gelled hair and light-colored clothing, but he had the most stunning blue eyes. They looked upward all the time with a surprised, happy expression. I'd remember eyes like that if I'd seen them before.

"Sorry, she was jumping, I didn't even see…" I stopped myself, watching as the guy fumbled with Beauty's harness.

"You can use the word see around blind people, you know. You just can't distract a guide dog in harness. There, girl, you're free."

Now Beauty yelped happily at me and I dropped to my knees in front of her, ignoring the guy's stupid comment. What was his problem, anyway? His horrible attitude seemed familiar too, like that guy from school we'd found on the street. What was his name again? Kyle? Beauty waved her tail at high speed, and lapped at my face and hands frantically, as though she couldn't lick up enough of me.

"Behave, girl," the guy said, tugging at the leash she still wore.

I felt my shoulders climb up my neck when he spoke to her like that. She's not my dog anymore. She's not my dog, I had to tell myself to stop from kicking him.

"Kyle Nicholson," a trainer called, checking something off on a clipboard. I froze. It was him. He used to wear black, and his sunglasses hid those eyes, but nothing could camoflage that attitude.

Kyle

Graduation II

This had to be the worst.

I wished that Beauty's foster owner hadn't come. To know that Beauty loved Elizabeth better than me—and yet sat tall in front of my feet, her back against my legs, no whimpering, no straining at the leash, perfectly loyal—I just wanted to give her more, to be more, to deserve that loyalty.

The evening dragged on as all nine of the smaller
hearing ear dogs and their partners got their graduation
certificates. Then the trainer showed a video and the
dogs barked at their partners when a phone rang on the
screen. Everyone laughed, and so did I—heh, heh. Even
though I just wanted to tell Elizabeth that I would love
this dog she'd given me with all that I could. That
maybe I wasn't the perfect owner yet, but that I could
learn to be.

When the video ended, the concert began.

Angela and I sang the Elvis "Hound Dog" song and
while I kept her leash under my feet, I felt and allowed
Beauty to raise herself and sway. Together we all got a
great round of applause. Who could resist a canine
Elvis? The number that Angela and I had written
together was scheduled for the grand finale. I wished we
could fast forward, but the trainers handed out certificates alternately to the foster families and the dog spon-
sors, drawing it all out with lots of appreciation speeches.

When would this ceremony part be over? Finally,
January called the girl's name: "Elizabeth, accepting for
the Kerr family." That was our finale cue. When
Elizabeth reached the front, the trainer was to signal us.
She touched my shoulder. I nodded to let January know
I was ready and she addressed Elizabeth.

"Kyle Nicholson wants you, especially, to hear this
song from him. Please take a chair."

I started strumming. Then I sang the first verse

about surfing in Waikiki and losing the beauty of the
sunset on the waves. I could picture it all in my head, a
pink and gold moment I'd never experience again.
Angela joined in on the chorus:

> *Because of you, I'm learning to*
> *Feel a different kind of Beauty.*
> *I cannot see, but I can be*
> *A person whole and full of Beauty.*
> *I love you the way I do, the way I can.*
> *Only you can help me. Without you, I can't be.*

Chopin, Fenway, Digby, King, Butterscotch—
Angela harmonized as I sang the names of all the other
dogs in the graduating class.

I didn't know what Elizabeth was thinking; I could-
n't see her face. All I could do was continue with the
other four verses and hope she would forgive me. For
thinking her dog had bitten me, for not being the perfect owner, for being nasty to her…the list stretched on.

I sang about how Beauty had kept me warm and put
a light inside me the night I'd collapsed on the street—
even though, before, dogs had inspired only terror.
About how she'd stopped me from walking in front of a
car. How I'd never loved any other dog before. And
then Angela joined me in the chorus after each verse.
When we hit the closing bar, I ad-libbed, making up a
verse: apologizing, explaining, begging. The whole graduating class joined in on the final chorus.

When we were finished, there was a long pause

before a huge wave of applause. At last, January thanked everyone and declared the graduation over.

I stood up and walked forward. "Find Elizabeth, girl." Beauty moved only slightly and then stopped. "Elizabeth? I really want to thank you for bringing up Beauty."

Total silence. Was she even there? Of course she was. Beauty wriggled in her harness and whined.

"Do you think maybe…that is to say, is there any way you think we could go for a walk sometime?… Or, do you by any chance like French fries with cheese and gravy? I mean, I just want you to stay in our lives."

More silence. I threw up my hands. It was just too hard talking to someone when you couldn't see or hear any reaction.

More silence. Then, "Have you ever tried Roller-blading?"

"Can't say I have. Why?"

"Because I think you'd like it just as much as surf-ing. Especially on this hill we have in the park. Would you take Beauty's harness off again?"

"For sure." Before I could bend over, I felt Elizabeth's arms around me, squeezing me tightly. I hugged back and heard Beauty bark. I smiled.

"Hold it right there, you two. I want to take your picture." My mother's voice. I heard the click of the camera. What did that remind me of? I saw it all again in my head: the tourists poised with their cameras along the beach at Waikiki, trying to capture forever an image of the sun melting into the ocean. And I could almost feel again that sense of balance I'd had as I'd stood up on the surfboard. In balance with life, even as it hurtled me forward to unknown destinations.

"One more, just in case," Mom said.

This moment, right now, was pink and gold too. I could feel the sun rise inside me again. And after Mom finished taking our picture, Elizabeth chatted with January about raising another puppy.

THE END